"*The Sunken Cathedral* is impressionistic, a book of drifting shadows and blazing clarity; Kate Walbert has written a gorgeous and moving requiem for a people and a city that are not yet lost. A magnificent achievement."

—LAUREN GROFF,
author of *Fates and Furies*

"*The Sunken Cathedral* is a gem of a novel—lyrical, ominous, and unexpectedly funny. Kate Walbert has somehow managed to write an elegy for a Manhattan that still exists."

—TOM PERROTTA,
author of *Little Children* and *The Leftovers*

"Kate Walbert sees in a manner that exalts the everyday into poetry and gives our deepest desires an unexpected and brilliant expression. She is among our very best writers, which *The Sunken Cathedral* makes abundantly clear."

—ANN PACKER,
author of *The Children's Crusade*
and *The Dive from Clausen's Pier*

"Kate Walbert is one of our very best writers, and *The Sunken Cathedral* is her finest, most original, and most absorbing novel yet. Its story of intersecting Manhattan lives is rich in history and memory and with dark intimations of the future, but is also steeped in Walbert's marvelous feel for life as we really experience it, from day to day, from moment to moment, in the surging rush of time."

—SAM TANENHAUS,
author of *The Death of Conservatism*

"A deeply human story, full of rich and complex characters." —J. Courtney Sullivan, *The Boston Globe*

*Praise for*

# THE

# SUNKEN
# CATHEDRAL

A *New York Times Book Review* Editors' Choice
A *San Francisco Chronicle* Best Book of the Year
A BBC Culture Top Ten Book
A *Tampa Bay Times* Best Book of the Year


"A keen observer of architecture, landscape, and culture, Walbert takes inspiration from Debussy's water music, referenced in the title and with impressionistic dabs of prose and subtle shifts of tone. Whether she is being technically exact or ingeniously play ful, above or below the (High) Line, Walbert's wistful glimpse of women reaching out during their last days of independence offers a penetrating look at New York and the world, post-9/11, post-Sandy, pre–the next disaster."

—*Publishers Weekly* (starred review)

"Strange storms haunt this novel, as does the fear that New York—the city now, the city's history—will soon be underwater. Elegant and elegiac."

—*Kirkus Reviews* (starred review)

"Hypnotic . . . An unconventional and unsettling novel with vivid imagery and passages of pure poetry."

—*Library Journal* (starred review)

"A sense of a remembered world that lives on just beneath the ever-changing surface is at the heart of Kate Walbert's stunning new novel, *The Sunken Cathedral*. A powerful elegy for a fading New York City and for the planet as a whole . . . Walbert writes with such precision that she's able to pack eighty years' worth of personal and world history—war, climate change, marriage, parenthood, friendship, death, grace, love, petty betrayal, and sudden violence—into a slim volume."

—J. Courtney Sullivan, The Boston Globe

"Insightful about the mysterious ways our lives play out . . . Rich . . . May remind readers of Virginia Woolf . . . Although Walbert never allows her narrative to dissolve into stream of consciousness, she manipulates time and space as though they were as viscous as oils. And she allows the central plot to drip off the edges of this canvas. That effect is structurally emphasized by footnotes that read like little prose poems of ineffable grace. . . . Stories shift as subtly as twilight into yet other stories."

—Ron Charles, The Washington Post

"Walbert packs everything into [a] series of braided narratives: deliciously human, memorable characters; the sensuous physical world; a tart omniscience shepherding a brisk pace. Best, she infuses The Sunken Cathedral with a sense of time's relentlessness: how it pools and eddies, drowns or sweeps away what once mattered—and how we respond to our arbitrary placement in it. . . . Time is deepened in these pages by commentaries or expansions in the form of long footnotes—a form I've rarely liked elsewhere but which works powerfully here. . . . Walbert's past oeuvre has notably examined the predicaments of women. She accomplishes that here again brilliantly, but this time her style allows easier entry, and her scope widens. An irresistible tone balances tenderness, excruciation, and vaudeville. . . . Sharp, richly imagined, The Sunken Cathedral serves—like much of Walbert's work—as a lovely manifesto: Attention must be paid."

—Joan Frank, San Francisco Chronicle

"Walbert, admirable for her willingness to experiment, is trying to tell—or show—us something. She has sought to give visual form to the fragmented nature of our existence, suspended between past and present, memories and associations forever intruding on fresh experience."

—Emily Eakin, The New York Times Book Review

"Walbert takes her remarkable technical prowess to a new level. . . . a beautiful tribute to a city that's continually in flux."
—Heller McAlpin, NPR

"Walbert is a writer with the power to alter your view of the world. . . . *The Sunken Cathedral* is an experience, a friend, an intellectual companion, a jewel with many facets . . . a carefully curated collection of words that the author has polished to a brilliant shine."
—Martha Sheridan, *The Dallas Morning News*

"Kate Walbert paints women's lives in indelibly rich and vibrant colors. . . . Walbert skillfully uses footnotes to tell some of the stories. These are not the miniature theses of a David Foster Wallace footnote, but undercurrents to the narrative, deeply personal stories. . . . Walbert conjures [the] past as she embodies the present, in shimmeringly lovely prose embedded with jewellike details."
—Colette Bancroft, *Tampa Bay Times*

"In *The Sunken Cathedral*, Kate Walbert renders an impressionistic portrayal of an imperiled New York, whose residents live with the threat of weather surges and terrorism in a city that is at once mythical and real . . . A brilliant allegory."
—Joseph Peschel, *St. Louis Post-Dispatch*

"Compelling . . . *The Sunken Cathedral* is both wise and beautifully written."
—Katherine Bailey, *The Philadelphia Inquirer*

"A brief book with limitless depth."
—Maggie Galehouse, *Houston Chronicle*

"Walbert gives us prose that is poetic, luscious, and utterly exquisite, while remaining both accessible and elusive. She also litters her story with footnotes . . . these tidbits add extra color to an already brilliantly vibrant mosaic . . . I haven't read a book this beautifully written since Ondaatje's *The English Patient*."
—Davida Chazen, *BookBrowse*

"Walbert is a keen transmitter of women's voices, from conforming suburban wives in the 1950s to British suffragettes during World War I. . . . Walbert tunes in to a complex chorus of female characters in contemporary Manhattan, a city recently altered by climate change, tragedy, and new wealth . . . the novel is strengthened by Walbert's use of footnotes, which allow her characters' thoughts to move freely from the present to the past, uncovering private or previously unshared memories. . . . Ambitious, elegiac, and occasionally funny, *The Sunken Cathedral* is an emotionally resonant story of people caught in a time of unease and change—and a striking portrait of the way we live now."

—Lauren Bufferd, *BookPage*

"Walbert's style calls to mind the work of John Banville."

—Eddie Joyce, *Washington Independent Review of Books*

"Walbert's taut novel touches on all that is now at risk in the city—whether from a cascade of water or a cascade of money."

—*Shelf Awareness*

"Walbert writes unlike anyone I've read before, imbuing each of her finely tuned sentences with stunning detail. Trust me: You won't ever have been more eager to read the footnotes in your life."

—*Bustle*

ALSO BY KATE WALBERT

*Where She Went*

*The Gardens of Kyoto*

*Our Kind*

*A Short History of Women*

# THE
# SUNKEN
# CATHEDRAL

- A NOVEL -

# KATE WALBERT

IOWA CITY
DISCARDED
from Iowa City Public library
SEP 2018
PUBLIC LIBRARY

Scribner

New York   London   Toronto   Sydney   New Delhi

SCRIBNER
An Imprint of Simon & Schuster, Inc.
1230 Avenue of the Americas
New York, NY 10020

This book is a work of fiction. Any references to historical events, real people, or real places are used fictitiously. Other names, characters, places, and events are products of the author's imagination, and any resemblance to actual events or places or persons, living or dead, is entirely coincidental.

Copyright © 2015 by Kate Walbert

All rights reserved, including the right to reproduce this book or portions thereof in any form whatsoever. For information, address Scribner Subsidiary Rights Department, 1230 Avenue of the Americas, New York, NY 10020.

First Scribner trade paperback edition March 2016

SCRIBNER and design are registered trademarks of The Gale Group, Inc., used under license by Simon & Schuster, Inc., the publisher of this work.

For information about special discounts for bulk purchases, please contact Simon & Schuster Special Sales at 1-866-506-1949 or business@simonandschuster.com.

The Simon & Schuster Speakers Bureau can bring authors to your live event. For more information or to book an event, contact the Simon & Schuster Speakers Bureau at 1-866-248-3049 or visit our website at www.simonspeakers.com.

Interior design by Jill Putorti

Manufactured in the United States of America

10  9  8  7  6  5  4  3  2  1

Library of Congress Control Number: 2014040854

ISBN 978-1-4767-9932-2
ISBN 978-1-4767-9936-0 (pbk)
ISBN 978-1-4767-9937-7 (ebook)

*For Rafael*

I

The water rushed the low bank, its first destruction the
unbinding of the strange bound sticks that had for years
appeared along the West Side Highway bike path, sticks criss
crossed atop stones stacked in ways that suggested they meant
something to someone. In an instant the water broke it all down,
the detritus swiftly clogging the already clogged drains as the
river rose—fast, there was pressure there, volume and shifting
tides, currents, swells—over the West Side Highway bike path,
flooding the recently resodded Hudson River Park, the roots of
its sycamores and maples, ornamental cherry and dogwood too
shallow to grip. The trees toppled and bobbed, knocking in a
surging logjam the limestone foundations of the once tenement
art galleries, the red-brick churches and garages, and too numerous to count glassy condo towers—each a flimsy envelope leak-
ing carbon, heat, cooled air in summer. Now, capable of resisting
nothing, their glass panes pop and shatter like so many bottles
lobbed to the sidewalk, the ones that remain reflecting the
darkening sky and the tempest of the day and the rising swirl
of water as the higher, richer tenants stand in black silhouette.

Helen puts her hands into the rush of water. She knows it

is unstoppable; ridiculously unstoppable. Too soon the famous buildings will buckle and go under just as easily as she did a little girl at the great waterfall at Great Falls. She went under in her daisy two-piece, her hard, pale body tight and smooth as the water that knocked her breath out, Great Falls too rough, her mother had warned. She could still hear her mother's warning somewhere far away, distant as church bells.

She had known all along, her mother was saying.

What the hell had they been thinking? her mother was saying.

What the hell had any of them been thinking?

# II

Simone had the idea: she might finish Henry's last canvas if she knew a little something—think of the poetic justice, the symmetry! Wasn't Roebling's widow the one who actually *built* the Brooklyn Bridge? She had read it, Simone said. She was sure she had. Marie had no clue but then again, things like this never interested her—details and dates, the particularities of history. She had only agreed to accompany Simone to Twenty-Seventh and Sixth, to the decrepit-looking building that housed the School of Inspired Arts, out of their long friendship or, rather, out of a certain habit of loyalty. Standing at the battered door, SCHOOL OF INSPIRED ARTS written in blue ink and Scotch-taped above an arrow that reads HERE, Marie hopes Simone will change her mind, hopes Simone will forget this plan and suggest home, though Simone persists, pressing the buzzer once and then again until someone releases the lock and she pushes in.*

---

*Before Marie's own husband, Abe, had passed, the couples did everything together: vacations with the children, New Year's Eve dinners, Sunday walks in Brooklyn, where, as the younger versions of themselves, they had lived among tenements and garment factories and untended walk-ups with

"Come on," Simone says, the elevator in the tiny vestibule predictably out of service, the handrail up the stairs worn and sticky—Simone commenting on the different smells—lasagna?—of the passing establishments until they reach the top, or sixth floor, the office of the School of Inspired Arts or, rather, its founding director, Sid Morris, his smock neatly folded on a metal chair, his small suitcase packed and ready at his feet. "In the unlikely event of an emergency," he says, ushering them in, smiling as if he'd been waiting all along and here they were.

Simone introduces herself, explaining to Sid Morris why they have come and how they have no artistic training, per se, but believe they might, even at this more advanced age—and here Simone clears her throat—be advised on the principles of color and composition. Marie stands a bit behind, trying to gauge whether Sid Morris considers them ridiculous old women in boiled wool coats and solid pumps or potential students or, oddly, both. They might be both, or other: schoolgirls in pleated skirts and white blouses, Peter Pan collars pressed and starched by mothers only dimly remembered as seamed stockings washed and hung to dry on the line, hairpins clenched in pursed lips. Blue eyes, Marie thinks now. Mother had blue eyes.

"In short," Simone says, Sid Morris standing and jingling what sounds like change in his pocket but what Marie will later learn is an enormous ring of keys, "we are happy to join a class,

---

impoverished front gardens—a statue of the Virgin Mary within a circle of begonia, a lone beach chair next to an American flag. It was in Brooklyn that Marie had first met Simone, in a weedy playground at the end of the boulevard Abe claimed went all the way to the Atlantic Ocean. The two were there every morning speaking French to the children as they pushed them on the swings, Simone's daughter, Katherine; Marie's little boy, Jules. French the children learned beautifully and then eventually refused to speak.

or participate in whatever way possible. You do, I should note, come *highly* recommended."

This Marie knows to be a bald-faced lie. Simone has found Sid Morris on the community pinup board in Chelsea amid the flyers advertising housekeepers and the guy who for years has promised, a bit hysterically, to teach you to "Speak Spanish like a Native!" She has a way, Simone, of flattering; arriving for their weekly dinner at the Galaxy diner (Friday, rice pudding) or a theater date (only musicals, their hearing) to marvel at Marie's dress or shoes—an old pair she dusted from her closet last minute. "But they're new! They simply are!"

"*Recommended,*" Sid Morris repeats.

"Highly," Simone says.

"Lovely word," Sid Morris says. "One of my favorites."

Sid Morris looks as Marie expected: unshaven face, tangle of eyebrows, beret for effect, and color smudged on his forehead. He's as old as they are, a bit stooped but otherwise compact, fit, even, so that calisthenics are likely involved—dumbbells, jumping jacks, perhaps even one of those lumbar belts.

"That and *reckoning, restorative,*" he says.

"The three *r*'s," Simone says.

Are they flirting? Marie thinks. She wouldn't be surprised.

"Tell you what, Miss Simone and—"

"Marie," Marie says. She forgot to introduce herself and Simone had barged ahead, anyway. Now the three stand in Sid's small office, the smell petrol and turpentine and cigarettes, the look nothing more than a metal desk shoved against a cinder-blocked wall and a chair of the kind more frequently found abandoned on side streets—TAKE ME I'M YOURS! Scotch-taped to its clawed leather seat. Above this a reproduction of a predictable Van Gogh—sunflowers—and an industry calendar, its days x-ed in the kind of monthly countdown found in certain workplaces. To what end? Marie thinks. *The* end? Sid Morris has already x-ed out his day and it is not yet noon.

"Pleasure," Sid Morris says, shaking her hand, his smile a line of stained teeth. He turns back to Simone and continues. "I don't often do this so late in the game. With beginners," he says, referring to Henry's canvas now offered for view: the Brooklyn Bridge, sketched in charcoal gray, the sky the background along with other unidentifiable forms: billows of smoke or possibly gathering thunderclouds. It would have been Henry's right to paint gathering thunderclouds, sick as he was, sick as he knew himself to be. Perhaps he cavorts in them now, in relief. He is in relief, Simone has said, not *dead*, exactly, but unseen; or did she say, It is a relief?

Oils a recent transition, Simone is explaining. He began with white, as white is everything when seen—whatever that means, it's something she read—and then introduced blues and reds, the shadow colors, he had called them, though one traditionally would think gray, she says.

"Uh-huh," Sid Morris says.

He expressed interest in shadows, Simone says, specifically the work of Turner, those soft colors. Would you call them soft colors? Turner's minimal palette. Could you call it a minimal palette?

Sid Morris stands back and crosses his arms, impatient. Where does he have to go? He has already x-ed off the day.

"Very well," he says, interrupting. "I have a Thursday group. We recently lost a few of our regulars—"

"I'm sorry," Simone says.

"They left town," Sid Morris says.

"Oh," Simone says.

"It's advanced," he says. "I mean in skill," he adds. "It might take some time to catch up. There's a model, that kind of thing."

"We're quick learners," Simone says.

"I don't doubt," Sid Morris says. He looks at Simone in a too-familiar way, as if he understands her intention to suggest something more magnificent. A certain gesture all it takes with Simone, who still sleeps with lotioned hands in yellow dishwater gloves, her hair set, eyebrows pencil-drawn just so: a GI wife. Henry—4th Infantry—had found her huddled in a coal cellar. Coaxed her out with a chocolate bar. He liked to tell the story: A feral cat, he would say. Lice. Scabies. Do you know scabies? Rhetorical question. Marie had also survived the war, that black, foul soap that left your scalp raw. But Henry liked to tell the story: how Simone, still a teenager, wore a dress of her mother's, silk, shreds, once her favorite green.


Thursday and Marie and Simone cast out again for the School of Inspired Arts, not so great a distance from Marie's brownstone in Chelsea, a fashionable neighborhood filled with gay men and dogs in stylish coats and today, due to the drizzle, matching booties. A Tibetan nanny pushes a plastic-sheathed stroller over the slick sidewalks, its rider a wide-eyed Caucasian baby, his mouth clamped on a pacifier. Marie links her arm in Simone's and the two, hunched with age, their hair tinted a prettier, pinker gray, make their slow way east and north.

Marie had been the most reluctant to leave Brooklyn, Abe insisting they could be pilgrims in Chelsea, where he had found the brownstone for cheap, an SRO with a Monticello banister— he a student of these things—intricate molding, tin ceilings, a deep backyard, and a stained-glass window where, if you craned a little, you had a view of the Empire State Building. On certain nights, looping his long arm around Marie's shoulders, he would pull her in to see the famous landmark through the stained glass, swearing that the spire—he always called it a spire, as if it were a church or holy place—looked even more magnificent seen through blue, or yellow. Years later, when the persons in charge began to light the spire itself—to save the birds, she had heard—Abe claimed he had known all along its need for color.

Behind them lived a piano teacher—Mrs. Stein. In the early summer evenings Marie and Abe would hear the single notes of the beginners from the parlor floor of Mrs. Stein's brownstone, windows open to the breeze, the beginners playing, then stopping, playing, then stopping, Mrs. Stein tapping their wrists with a ruler—that kind of woman, maybe Stern, in fact, maybe she was Mrs. Stern—instructing them to begin, again. Always to begin, again, the single notes, the same pattern, memorized by every child. She and Abe listened and watched as Jules dug in his sandbox beneath the cherry that finally grew, though at first it seemed it would never, stuck in the mud, a sapling she had bought from one of the wholesalers on Twenty-Eighth: the blossoms a promised pink. Abe built Jules a sandbox at its roots and in late spring would shake a spindly limb and make pink rain.*

The model, a too-thin girl with a tattoo of a crucifix on her arm and a serpent up her backside, drops her pose to stare as the two finally take their places—late, again, and this their fifth week—at their easels in the half circle, the other students mostly middle-aged, raincoated, scarfed, a collection of wet smells, fur-

---

*Marie finds it almost unbearable that Abe is dead and she is alive. When the telephone rings, she often waits to listen again to his voice on the answering machine explain to the caller that no one is home, and to please leave a message.

tive cigarettes, coffee. Among them a pharmacist on his lunch hour, a red-stitched Duane Reade across the pocket of his lab coat; a black-haired woman, Helen, with four daughters, who, in a past life, she has told them during Friendly Break, labored as an art historian; a young man who never smiles.

They unlock their tackle boxes as the model settles back, arms over head, eyes closed, lying on the broken-down divan pushed so close to the radiator Marie worries it might burst into flames; she can only imagine the egress. To her left, Helen appears absorbed in her submerged skyscrapers—the Woolworth Building, Rockefeller Center, the once Twin Towers—fish circling their windows. Did this have to do with global warming? The rising sea level? A foot before the end of the next decade! Jules told her just last week. "And you're in flood zone A!"

Marie has no idea. She thinks to ask Helen but she has learned that talking is strictly forbidden before Friendly Break, Sid Morris wandering among them like a trainer among poised seals, stopping to make a suggestion or tap a shoulder or once, even, to stand very close to Simone and whisper something Marie could not make out. In the background, classical music plays from a paint-splattered radio, the New York station with the ancient announcer more frequently heard in doctors' waiting rooms and other places where signs prohibit the use of cell phones—the last bastions of Beethoven or Chopin or, on racier days, Shostakovich.

Marie stares at her canvas: five weeks of work and still almost nothing. She thinks of Jules chalking the entire universe in just days: planets on the front stoop then suns and moons on the sidewalk, forests, magical animals, drawing until dark, when she would open the front door and ask where he had landed. California, he always said, given his interest in Disneyland. Once a late-night rainstorm washed it all away, or most of it, leaving Jules predictably heartbroken. Jules of the pink rain; Jules of the faint of heart. Jules crying, again. He had been planning something, his fierce little face, red-cheeked, pale, the lashes of his eyes wet with tears. Does he have a scraped knee? A gash? She blows on the raw skin, lightly, not even enough to extinguish a candle's flame, and he closes his beautiful eyes and holds his breath.

"Marie!"

"Yes?" Has she been sleeping? She sits in front of the easel, tackle box now at her feet, the tubes of paint and brushes purchased at the art store on Twenty-Third Street after the first class, a discount for mentioning the famous Sid Morris, who suddenly looms behind her, too close, breathing. She smells the strong tobacco. Let the sonsofbitches arrest me, he had said; let the ghost of Bloomberg kiss my carcinogenic ass.

"Explain," he says.

"What do you mean?" she says.

"I'd like to hear your thoughts," he says.

The entire class waits to hear her thoughts.

"These are the suns," she begins.

"Plural?"

"It's a universe."

"Oh."

"And these are some planets and I skipped them because it got too hard and I'm working on the forest and animals."

"This is a deer?"

"A rabbit."

"Right."

Duane Reade shifts on his stool. Marie understands that he is not so absorbed in his own work—that none of them are—as not to be listening. She looks out at them but they are pretending.

"You said we could do anything," Marie says.

"I did," Sid Morris says, touching her shoulder, lightly, quickly. "And you may," he adds, moving on to Duane Reade.

"Speaking of rabbits," Helen whispers, leaning toward Marie to take a look, though this, too, is strictly forbidden. "My British granddaughter has a jumping rabbit. She enters it in contests. The craziest thing," she says. "It's a new sport, rabbit jumping. They make them go over these tiny poles, like horses."

"Really?" Marie says.

"God's truth," Helen says, turning back to her own canvas, where, it seems, she has decided to introduce magical creatures, or so this one appears, hunched, winged, its beak a weedy orange. It is perched on one of her toppled buildings as if a cormorant on a craggy rock, oblivious to the legions submerged.

# III

The mothers, dressed for exercise, gather on the steps of Progressive K‑8. Stephanie G. at the center, forty‑five, give or take, her hair in short braids, dandelions woven into the bands—Elizabeth sees her and sidesteps but too late.

"Elizabeth!" Stephanie G. calls. "Elizabeth!"

How had she agreed to the idea at all? Now Stephanie G. blocks her path, clearly determined to see the vision fulfilled: Who We Are stories line the hallways of Progressive K–8 like so many snowflake cutouts in winter, each sincere and beautiful and excruciatingly heartbreaking for reasons Elizabeth cannot name and does not want to examine. The idea had grown out of the school's pledge for better communication by way of stronger community, dialoguing through dialogue, something like that, one of those tautologically challenged declarations beloved by their new interim head of school—Dr. Constantine—an elderly woman whose early advocacy of sexual education in pre-K put her on the academic map. If everyone could share their roots, or dig down to their roots, or expose their roots the school might come together in a grand way, or at least in a way that would increase the parent participation in the annual fund drive.

It had all been outlined in an e-mail: IMPORTANT ANNOUNCE-
MENT FROM DR. CONSTANTINE, which Elizabeth opened expecting to
read of another outbreak of nits on a fifth grader's scalp or an
additional plea for vigilance when patrolling the City blocks
after pickup. This, Elizabeth's favorite parental responsibility:
mothers and the occasional bemused father wandering Bleecker
Street in pairs regardless the weather, dressed in bright orange
vests and carrying heavy walkie-talkies, a bit over-the-top, yet
still: vigilance must be maintained, Dr. Constantine stressed,
especially in the event of a What If.*

Last month Elizabeth had patrol duty with a woman
whose son was in first grade, a woman tall and thin with dark,
New York hair and glasses suggesting a love of books or at
least a graduate degree in the humanities. The two had wandered the block greeting other mothers they knew, nodding to
clusters of students and telling them to get along, eyeing any
stray man who seemed not to have a destination in mind, their
hands gripping the walkie-talkies just in case they needed to
call back in to, whom? Dr. Constantine? Central control? The
crackle of static had felt comforting, as was the idea of a direct
link to someone who might allay her more general fears: Dirty
bomb a hoax, the voice would whisper; organic beef as good
as grass-fed.

But this e-mail had a different message:

What's Your Story? it read. We're asking the Progressive

---

*What Ifs were favorites of Dr. Constantine's, who often opened her monthly
*Cappuccinos with Constantine* by tossing What Ifs to the crowd: What If an
earthquake were to knock out the power grid? What If an outbreak of avian flu
occurred during a blizzard? What If I never do my homework? Elizabeth's son,
Ben, newly thirteen, now liked to throw back at her, What If I refuse to get out
of bed?

K–8 Community to participate in a 3-E endeavor to Enliven, Engage, and Enlighten with Who We Are stories. Everyone has one: Great-Uncle Vic worked as a tailor for Chiang Kai-shek; Grandmother Sanchez escaped from Castro's Cuba. Whatever it is, we want to know! And please, include pictures!

"So, who are we?" Ben asked that night at the dinner table.

"What?" Elizabeth said, distracted by the amount of cheese he had stuffed in his taco.

"Dr. Constantine said we were supposed to remind you," Ben said, negotiating a bite. "I'm reminding you."

"Oh, that," she said, turning to her husband, who scooped the meat with a spoon and whose pale, delicate fingers, long and tapered, looked as if he should be playing a musical instrument. "What?" Pete said. "What are we talking about?"

"We're supposed to write a Who We Are story," Elizabeth said. "You know, where we come from, how we ended up here. They're asking everyone to do it. One of those community things."

Pete looked at her as if not comprehending. She had noticed this more and more about him, these brief synapses—hamster trances, Ben called them—and wondered if it had to do with his not sleeping, or maybe the hours he spent sitting at a desk staring at small numbers moving across a computer screen or on the device held in his palm. Perhaps he was waiting for his wife and son to morph into something else, for the trading feed to begin its loop across the bottom of the page: information, statistics, the rise and fall of the stock exchange; or possibly he hoped the text might offer links to other sites, sites that would explicate his family's deeper, troubling mysteries—his wife's increasing restlessness, his son's unpredictable moods.

"My ancestors were Welsh," Pete said. "You could write about that. The Welsh are interesting."

"I thought Holland," Elizabeth says.

Pete shrugs. "Somebody sailed from Rotterdam before the Revolution, but then there was also something about Wales. Nobody really knows."

"If you were a girl you could be a member of the DAR," Elizabeth says to Ben. "That's kinda cool."

Ben looks from one to the other then takes a tremendous bite of his taco, tomatoes and cheese and lettuce shreds raining down on his plate, and to the side of the plate onto the good tablecloth.

"Promise me you won't take your first date out for tacos," Elizabeth says.

"I promise I won't take my first date out for tacos," Ben says, his mouth full. When did he get so large, so ungainly, so hairy? He is all arms and legs, as if he can't even fit into his chair. They sit on the chairs she and Pete bought in Mexico, right after their wedding. The chairs have rattan seats the cat has destroyed and are grease-stained and worn but when she looks at them she thinks of Pete speaking broken Spanish, attempting to bribe someone at the post office in Oaxaca to mail them freight.

"We could write how we had tacos on our first date," Elizabeth says to Pete, feeling suddenly expansive, young; she might be twenty-eight; she might be walking on that beach in Mexico, the one where they stayed before leaving for Oaxaca, where the chickens and seagulls followed them for crumbs. They were eating galletas; they were leaving a trail in case they got lost. "We could write that when I took the first bite he wondered if he could have a second date, much less spend the rest of his life with me."

"I did wonder that," Pete says.

"First date?" Elizabeth says.

"What did we do?" Pete says.

"Chinese," Elizabeth says.

"Right," Pete says. "I was thinking egg roll."

"Chinatown," Elizabeth says.

"Right, right. You had the spicy braised fish," he says, though she didn't—at the time she refused to eat anything with scales.

"And then we went to hear music," she says.

"Muddy Waters," Pete says.

"Willie Dixon," Elizabeth says. "And ate those little balls with the toothpicks for dessert. They were too sweet. They're always too sweet."

"I moved into your mother's apartment. It was above Sherm's—" Pete says to Ben.

"Sherman's was an upscale diner and all day Sunday you smelled all the delicious—" says Elizabeth.

"Sausage."

"Your father didn't have a dime. We never ate out again," Elizabeth says.

"One time your mother found this stray dog and asked the waiters if they had any leftover sausage—"

"Oh God!"

"For the dog," Pete says. He smiles, remembering.

Ben has his eyes covered, head on the table, or the pretty tablecloth. "Should I be writing this down?" he says.


Two fathers sprint past Stephanie G., their jacket tails flying as if they can't wait to get the hell to their jobs. Certain days the fathers turn out in impressive numbers, walking their young children to school, looking handsome and freshly showered, many in well-cut suits and a few in jeans and bomber jackets, good shoes, and one or two in grungy clothes. The fathers must exercise at different times, maybe earlier in the morning before they have showered, or possibly at night or possibly not at all, though in general the fathers look more physically fit than the mothers and, truth be told, Elizabeth thinks, younger. How could you account for this? How can you possibly reconcile the great inequities of gender—coupled with the perversions of age and the general randomness of everything? Who could you call to complain? Or is it *whom*?

"Elizabeth?" Stephanie G. is saying. "Are you with me?"

"Oh, sorry," Elizabeth says, too quickly. "Yes, of course. Absolutely. What?"

"I was saying we're trying to get one hundred percent participation. It's part of the General Mandate. I saw you signed up for the Environmental Committee, too," she says. "Of course there's no saying you can't do both." Stephanie G. cocks her head to one side. She actually looks cute in braids, Elizabeth thinks. Maybe how she looked as a child, eager, happy, always ready to include the third girl or stand up to the bully. She clerked for a Supreme Court justice until she had her second son—now there are four—worked as the editor of the law review, supported her alcoholic mother, et cetera, et cetera. When she had started putting dandelions in her hair Elizabeth can't quite remember, though it may have been right around the time Stephanie G. cochaired the third-grade flower drive. Those days you would never see her without a potted plant in her hands or a sprig of something behind her ear.

"I mean unless you want to," Stephanie G. says. "If you want to, that would be terrific."

"No, I'm good," Elizabeth says. "That sounds great," she adds, not quite understanding what she's agreed or not agreed to. She had joined the Environmental Committee after the e-mail went

out that every parent was expected to serve on a volunteer committee or two, given the lackluster response to the all-volunteer
volunteer committees. She had a vision of herself with the rest of
the committee in gloves and comfortable boots, the sun streaming down as they tended to the delicate morning glories entwin-
ing the chain-link fence that guarded the children from running
off the roof playground, or clipped a potted hedgerow or two,
possibly, or watered a copse of birch, birch mostly foreign to the
City, especially downtown, but for a while she could picture it:
the kindergartners tricycling through the birch, their little legs
turning the wheels as fast as they could, careering around the
roof playground as if they had suddenly found themselves in a
magic forest. The birch might even mute the sounds of traffic
and attract the wildlife from farther north, near Central Park, the
families of squirrel and raccoon and even otter.

"Anyway, there's no rush," Stephanie G. is saying, "though
we do hope to get everything in by the end of the year."

"All right," Elizabeth says. "We'll think of something," she
says.

"Wonderful!" Stephanie G. says, striding down the steps and
disappearing into the band of suitably stretched women. They
will run from here a few blocks north, across Fourteenth Street,
then up the West Side Highway bike path as far as they can go,
some of them, even, sprinting the GW Bridge to the Palisades,
these the most determined, the marathoners, the ones who,
heads down, feet sneakered, push and push their tired hearts, as
that runner once did to warn the Athenians of the Spartans, or
maybe it was the other way around.

# IV

Simone's talk turns to Sid Morris, as it will, to the awkward way he holds his hands, to his fingers in particular, slender, pale, as if he has been instructed to keep his wrists up and they've been drained of blood, to the way he sniffles when he has something important to say, or what he believes to be important, to his habit of suggesting, before anyone begins, that they sit with their own palms up, fingers up, eyes closed, and relax their toes in a kind of collective meditation.

"Toes!" Simone says, though she's delighted. He liked the progress of Henry's Brooklyn Bridge; he liked her sweater; he liked what she had to say about Cézanne's principle of certainty, something Sid Morris imparted last class during Friendly Break. Over the past few months they have learned much about Sid Morris during Friendly Break, how he worshiped at the altar of the Ashcan School, how he was raised somewhere near Coney Island; how he lived in a studio apartment, an only child, with aged parents; and how, as a boy punk, he would take a nickel subway to the West Side, where the banana boats docked and you had to watch the spiders, big as your fist, tarantulas that would come up from Panama or Brazil or wherever the fuck it was they grew bananas, but you could always earn enough unloading to get in the pinup clubs that have long since closed or the bars of Hell's Kitchen, which really was, then, Hell. Not like now: before, Sid Morris would say: tenements and immigrants, the teaming masses yearning to be free, fighting like cats in a bag, sonsofbitches most though some good souls who moved among them, administering. No one now knows from poor, he said.

They have learned the things Sid Morris says he cannot forget: that he did nothing when a boy in his gang tormented another into falling from a fourth-floor window, that he cheated on his wife and was a rotten father to his only child, foolishly named Veritas; that he killed not one Communist in the war but shot himself, instead; that he skipped his mother's funeral for a party.

But he is not alone; there are other old cowards still hanging on in the East Village, in Chelsea, on the Lower East Side, men who frolicked with the likes of Rauschenberg and Warhol, their aged companions—once ingenues—still painting spheres, squares, a circle in their rent-controlled studios, their arthritic hands claw-curled to the brush.

Beauty! Sid Morris said, addressing the dirty windows that looked out to the alley where, on certain Thursdays, the smell up from the Chinese restaurant across the street reached a point you could almost taste. Beauty! he said.

"He *is* talented," Simone is saying. "I mean, not *hugely* so, but in the way one must be in order to teach."

"Yes," Marie says.

"He's got an interesting way of speaking."

She hasn't noticed. "I know," she says.

"I wonder if he stuttered as a child. I bet he stuttered. So many of them did."

Time was Marie might have asked Simone what she meant, exactly—so many children stuttered? Boys? Boys named Sidney?—but age has undermined the urgency of these questions, or made them less pressing, somehow; most things unexplainable anyway—words too quickly fall away, disappear; where, she isn't sure, but they are suddenly gone; language jittery, unsustainable. Connections lost. This is what has plagued her most about Abe's death—not so much the death of Abe, but the death of all Abe knew: his books, his lifetime of asking, his thoughts, his memories, all this and everything else, their yellow kitchen with each object in its place, carefully mannered, intricate, ornate though not rich, more historical or, rather, well loved—objects inherited from Abe's relatives in Philadelphia, silver a museum or a library collection would want to catalog though the value never interested him: it was the archaeology of the things, he would say, the history—the watchmaker's insignia, the fleur-de-lis crest. A fortune sat on these shelves. Even Very Grand on her wire in their bedroom, painted by some somebody known for portraiture, posed against her Victorian wallpaper, arms crossed, challenging, as if she'd rather be anywhere else, a wrap—was it then called a wrap?—around her pale, regal shoulders.*

"Marie?" Simone says.

"Yes?"

---

*After Abe's death she had hauled Very Grand to the basement, impossible to look at, impossible to remember Abe constantly rewriting her biography: a bad match with her first husband—a military man stationed somewhere in Egypt or, possibly, Algeria. She loved the blue of the sea but didn't like the heat and so left, Abe said, much to the despair of the children, whom she had abandoned without a moment's hesitation or, rather, only a moment's: she had been a debutante in Newport and then the wife of a scion; or a woman who dressed as a man to wander the markets of Zanzibar. In less than a day, Marie had hauled Very Grand back up the basement stairs to hang her in her old place, apologizing to the hollow air of the impossibly empty bedroom. "I'm sorry," she had said. "You can stay."

"You're daydreaming," Simone says.

"Hmm?"

"I said, the stew was delicious; you used fennel."

"Cumin."

"It tastes better than ever."

"Thank you."

Marie stands so abruptly the wooden chair wobbles. She gathers the plates and carries them to the sink. Where am I? she thinks: then, the yellow kitchen: the view: the darkening back garden. Beyond young families sleep in the taller building—a dull, white-bricked modern, twenty-some floors of windows in a checkerboard square, their lights a tic-tac-toe or random puzzle although the insomniac on the ninth floor remains as constant as the North Star. In a matter of hours they had torn down Mrs. Stern's brownstone and the others: the one with the window boxes, the one with the honeysuckle that grew over the roof, the wrecking ball the size of a boulder, and the sound so loud. Marie dries her hands slowly but Simone's coat is already over her shoulders.

"He asked me to coffee," Simone says, absently, as if distracted by a small loop of thread at her wrist. No doubt she waits, listening for the sharp intake of breath or whatever else she imagines Marie might do in response, the squeal, the handclap. What does she expect?

"And what did you say?" Marie asks, knowing.

Simone leans into her, her hand cold from the leaky, original windows, dry as dust against Marie's cheek. "You're very funny, my friend," she says. "I'll call you tomorrow."


It is difficult for Marie to sleep. She lies in bed with a book, a new one—all the rage—she must read in the large-print edition, the book too heavy to hold. Someone else's life around her neck, an albatross, someone who neither knows her nor would care to know her; a complete stranger and yet here she reads of the stranger's education, the stranger's first loves. There are photographs, too, an album of them in the middle of the book: a little girl clasps her mother's hand, their eyes similarly dark; a broad father stands behind wearing a bowler hat. Grandparents, she presumes. A horse. A table of smart-looking people, women in thick lipstick and strapless dresses and men in shirtsleeves, a club somewhere in Paris or, possibly, Berlin. History. Records. Refugees. Are the children beneath the table or sleeping on a mountain of furs in the ladies' room? Survivors all or, maybe, not—they dissolve at the touch, or will, eventually; they burst into flames with a single match. They melt to soap. She could burn this thick volume for warmth, she could eat the paper, make paper soup.

Over the mantel, Very Grand stares out at a distant point, her wrap around her pale shoulders, her elegant ankles cracked, the paint flaking: paint on plywood, perhaps. Difficult to tell: she's splitting apart, Very Grand: fissures span her skin, a delicate net on her hands, her face. And on her cheeks a new, flushed pink, as if Very Grand might be running a fever.

Marie gets out of bed and walks down the narrow hallway to the kitchen. She sits at her round table facing the back garden and the now-grown cherry, or rather the snow that outlines its bare branches, the snow that weighs it down to almost breaking. Winter and the branches breaking—it is very old for a cherry and they are ornamental, after all; they don't last forever.

A full moon—perhaps the cause of her restlessness—lights the snow white. Across the way the apartments are black as black, turned off, mostly, except for the ninth floor. The movie star's cat balances on the high fence that divides his backyard from hers—Roscoe, she remembers. The cat. The movie star bought the brownstone from her friends who moved to Florida after the last storm. She's had a phone call or two from them since, checking in after new disasters. They listen to Abe's instructions to leave a message and then they do. Are you okay? Do you need anything? Can we help?

"I survived the Blitz," she might tell them. "This is only weather," she might say, though she knows they are being kind.

She watches Roscoe balance on the high fence, his tail quivering, his shadow cast onto the snow like a black cardboard cat against the whiteness. The day the movie star moved in he knocked on her front door and asked if she had seen his cat, Roscoe. "Is he lost?" she had said. He was not so handsome in real life, his skin drawn back by one procedure or another, acne scars from a no doubt troubling adolescence. He wore a paperboy's hat and a T-shirt that said BITE ME.

"Obviously," he said.

Through the narrow gaps in the distant skyscrapers the Empire State Building has been turned off. To save energy, she knows, damn the birds. Now its spire is a dark outline of black; clouds, what clouds there are, wispy, angry, circling it like released Furies in the brightness of the moon.

My word, Marie thinks. What will they talk about?

# V

Marie serves the leftover stew, better days old, they both agree, and sherry. A sunny afternoon and the snow, still white in the backyard save pigeon scrawls and Roscoe's paw prints zigzagging in a hunter's trail, melts and drips from the back gutters, a ping ping ping sound they hear through the open kitchen windows. So bright this noonday light on the yellow walls; Marie never tires of it. As a little girl she dreamt she would live on a rooftop, or perhaps in a greenhouse. Now her bedroom faces south, better for Very Grand, Abe had said, though lousy for traffic. Oh well. There wasn't so much traffic then, not like now, with the tourists and the tourists. She's not heard this much French, she joked to Jules, since France!

"It would be easier for both of us," Jules says. "I wouldn't worry, you wouldn't need to look after yourself."

"I'm fine, darling. I have Simone. I have the butcher around the corner. I'm fine."

"Are you?" he says.

She would like to sprout wings and fly to him, like in that children's story where Mother is everywhere. What was that one? She flies to him and in his sleep he will not push her away, complain; she strokes his hair as she would when he felt feverish. She blows on his eyelids, tucks the blankets tight. Tighter, he says, in his sleep or maybe he has waked and sees her. He's a feverish boy and Mother is here and she will stay until he sleeps, again. Then she flaps home but first she circles the Empire State Building, resting on its spire, balancing as she deciphers the grid of the City to see where Abe has gone. Is this where Abe has gone? He loved it so. Maybe she will find him here. Maybe she will find them all, Mother and Father and Rose and Sylvie. Little Ernest with his spectacles, his pudgy hands and arms too short to reach the family sugar bowl she knew the hiding place of though she would never tell.*

"A little boy," Marie says.

"What?" Simone says. She puts down her fork. "Who?"

"I'm sorry," Marie says. "I was thinking."

"Were you listening? I was saying about Sid. Did you hear that?"

"What?"

"He's asked me now to *dinner*."

"Yes?"

*"Dinner."*

"I heard."

"I said I'd think about it. I didn't want to seem too eager. I don't really know anything about him," Simone says.

---

*Mother had once been a teacher. Rose and Sylvie had once been beauties; Marie had once jump-roped; Ernest had once been a little boy; they had all once gone on the train to the circus in Paris and bought sugar sticks in lemons and sucked the sweet juice and watched as a monkey climbed a man and took off his toupee and put it on his own funny monkey head.

"No," Marie says.

Simone sits back, scrapes her plate. She looks at Marie in the way she will at times, as if Marie is already a ghost, transparent. "Jules called my Katherine. Apparently he's worried. Thinks you shouldn't be rambling around this house on your own."

"Not to mention its property value," Marie says, immediately wishing she had not. Out back Roscoe stalks one of the pigeons in the flock beneath her bird feeder. Sparrows, too, an occasional brave cardinal, blue jay; once even a Baltimore oriole though Abe said impossible. But she had seen it: a flash of bright orange and black perched high in the neighbor's mulberry, its call unlike anything she had ever heard before. The bird sang its heart out, she told Abe. You should have heard, she told him. It sang like nothing.

The sun lights a square shadow across the snow, a box to climb down to, to fall into, or perhaps a box in which to hide.

"I guess Katherine mentioned our class. I've told her about Sid. You know how she asks questions. Anyway, you didn't?"

"What?"

"Our class. You didn't say anything to Jules?"

"It was going to be a surprise. The painting."

"Oh that's right."

"It has some significance."

"I remember."

"And yours?"

"Sid says I am beginning to develop an eye."

Simone laughs and the pigeons take flight or simply rearrange, as is the case with pigeons.

"So you're going to say yes?" Marie says.

"To Sid?" Simone says, as if that's a question. "What have I got to lose?"

# VI

"We're supposed to include a photograph," Elizabeth says to Ben and Pete. The dishwasher runs in the quiet cycle and they're sitting at the kitchen table drinking tea. Ben's pointy elbows rest on either side of his mug and he slouches in his chair. Near him the cat balances on his math book and he scratches her belly, which she turns to him, expectant.

"How about the one from Hawaii?" Pete says.

"Ben wasn't born," Elizabeth says.

"No way. He was always born," Pete says.

"Hah, hah," Ben says.

"I was thinking one of the ones from California," Elizabeth says.

"Forget it," Ben says.

"They're good," Elizabeth says.

"They sucked," Ben says.

"Don't say *suck*," Elizabeth says. "Say *they were terrible*."

"They were terrible," Ben says.

The radio alarm switches on, as it will every evening at 7:30 despite their best efforts to undo the setting.

"Let's write we have a ghost in the house," Ben says. "The ghost of the Old Lady's husband."

"Don't call her the Old Lady," Elizabeth says. "Her name is Mrs. Frank. Marie Frank. You can probably call her Marie now. She wouldn't mind. We've lived in her house since you were a baby."

"Duh," Ben says.

"Don't say *duh*," Elizabeth says.

"Maybe he lives in the radio," Pete says.

"Who?" Elizabeth says.

"The ghost of Marie's husband," Pete says.

"Abe," Elizabeth says. "Abraham Lincoln Frank. Isn't that great? She was a refugee and he was a professor: the refugee and the professor. That would be a good story."

The radio is set to a religious station of some sort, the announcer speaking about one of the gospels.

Elizabeth stomps across the floor to flick it off and the cat jumps to the counter and knocks over a water glass and Ben falls out of his Mexican chair to land with a thud on the floor.

"Enough!" Elizabeth says.

Ben lies there for a while in his soccer shorts and high kneesocks, his legs splayed like a giant sea creature, mottled pink skin and black hair. Elizabeth wouldn't be surprised if he suddenly sprouted something.

"What's for dessert?" he finally says, unmoving.


The Mexican chairs were lined in two neat rows, as if expecting company. They were simple, straight-backed chairs, several of them painted bright colors—orange, green, blue, yellow—but others not painted at all, others bare wood. These were the ones Elizabeth liked the best; they had already bought many things in Mexico—tablecloths, candleholders, silver jewelry for relatives—all the things kept in the special bag they had brought with them for purchases. It seemed crass but also okay: the things were beautiful and cheap, and they were young and poor. The Mexican chairs would cost a fortune to ship home, Pete said; they were out of their league.

Pete and Elizabeth had been in Oaxaca for several days, staying at the convent near the center square where every night men and women danced on raised platforms and tourists milled about, eating various desserts made from flan and listening to guitars and drinking tequila. Pete and Elizabeth also drank tequila, as well as some of the other liquor they loved; and they also listened to guitars and watched as the men and women danced on raised platforms. One night, in a restaurant, Elizabeth waited as a little yellow canary hopped off its perch and chose a tiny scroll with her fortune. The old woman who carried the cage with the canary said the bird could tell fortunes, that the bird would hop off its perch and choose a fortune and that the bird would be right. Elizabeth waited and listened as the woman took the little scroll from the bird and read her fortune and Pete translated, as best he could, what the woman said: You will make your own destiny, he said. You will find your own path. Then something I don't know, he said.

You don't know? Elizabeth said. That's a fortune? Elizabeth had said but still, she remembered it.

I want those chairs, she told Pete later in the room. They lay in the bed in the heat unclothed. They were trying to get pregnant and so made love as often as possible, but the flan had not agreed with her on this evening, so on this evening, they lay in bed next to one another but did not touch.

What? Pete said.

Those chairs, she said. Those chairs are my destiny.

Your destiny is chairs? Pete said; he had propped himself up on one elbow and looked down at her, his expression the one she loved most on him, when he seemed unsure whether she was joking or not, his mouth slightly skeptical. Plus, he had his vacation beard, which she also loved, and wore the thin gold necklace she had found at one of the outdoor markets that lined the streets, a necklace with a tiny crown charm Pete said was not a crown but was a symbol that had to do with the Incas; still, she liked the idea of her husband wearing a crown, she said, which by all rights would make her a queen.*

The canary told me, she said.

Pete touched her then on her stomach; he had slid his hand down the length of her stomach and then felt his way around.

Please, sweetheart, she said. I'm too sick.


The next day they went back to the chairs. Each had been carved out of wood, and on the back of them someone had whittled a sun, its expression different depending on the chair, but a sun on every one, regardless. She preferred the unfinished ones, she said to the woman selling the chairs.

No good, the woman said. They need protection.

I'll oil them, she said. Tell her I'll oil them, she said to Pete.

Pete repeated something to the woman, who only shook her head.

––––––––––––––

*Pete would never be mistaken for a jewelry man: She had met him at college years ago, where he rode a ratty pink bicycle and bought his books used at the Book Exchange. They were in Dostoyevsky together, though he remembered it as Nietzsche, his copy of The Possessed so illegible with the previous owner's comments—irony? metaphor? simile? synecdoche?—that Pete asked if he could borrow hers. She liked the frayed flannel of his collar. She liked how he bit his fingernails to the quick and rolled his own cigarettes. She liked, even, that he worked on Saturday and Sunday at Tech Library, alphabetizing the card catalog.

She's pretty clear she wants you to buy a painted one, Pete
said. What about the green?

I want the bare ones, Elizabeth said. Tell her we'll pay.

All right, Pete said. Keep your pants on.

Pete repeated something to the woman. She looked at Elizabeth, her face creased and burnt, a scarf wrapped around her
head and knotted.

It was a prophecy, Elizabeth said. It was the prophecy of the
yellow bird, she said. The woman smiled, her teeth white and
strong. She nodded as if she understood, and Elizabeth, somewhat abruptly, pulled one of the unpainted chairs out of its row
and plunked herself down. This one, she said to Pete. We'll get
the set, she said.


That night they line the chairs against the wall of their room
in the old convent, the chairs beneath the tiny ivory crucifix,
Christ painted on with some kind of vegetable dye, or possibly carved, the artist careful to nick the places where the nails
were hammered and dot each with a tiny speck of red. The ceiling is very high, and as Pete thrusts into her, lost, she pictures
herself floating above the bed, above the chairs, floating in the
dark space between the limits of the light and the ceiling. There
are kings and queens in the chairs, and all manner of religious
heretics and slaves; there are the martyrs they have read about
at every location, the ones whose names Pete can magically
recall—Sebastian the Beheaded, Epiphania the Exalted—and
the hermits and eunuchs and saints of the early Renaissance,
the popes; there are members of her family, too, and the constant ghost of Molly; there is her mother, Doreen, whose love
is blue and whose anger turns her a glowing, pulsing, muscle
red. There are women she has only heard of—grandmothers and

great-grandmothers, some who were carried west against their will, across great oceans they were convinced were inhabited by unfathomable demons, and others who came willingly, if not docilely, their feet too sore to complain, their spirits crushed— wives of clergymen, daughters of patriarchs; she has no idea who they were, or are, though they line up beneath her as if Russians queuing for bread.

She lies in the crux of Pete's arm, his vacation beard sharp against her, his breathing fast. She knows at this moment they have created a life; she can feel it, she can read it, almost, as if it were written on the tiny scroll, the little canary hopping off its perch to pluck the one scroll from the tight bunch of scrolls it must choose from.

The lights are out by the time Pete comes to bed. She's been reading, she says. Good night, she says.

Pete turns to kiss her then rolls over on his side. "I thought of one," Pete says into the dark. "Ben's swim meet last summer. The championship. It's of all of us, remember?"

"Okay," she says.

"I'll find it tomorrow," he says.

"Great," she says.

"You look beautiful in it," he says.

"I don't remember," she says; then she says nothing, just thinks, listening to Pete and the slowing-down breathing of Pete falling asleep. Maybe this is a night when he has cleared his mind—the tacos, Ben suggesting Scrabble after dinner. She watched as the two of them played and it was simple; for a moment, it was simple and she did not feel the speeding up of urgencies or sense the lengthening shadow of the past; she did not seek the accumulating dark at the limits of the light.

# VII

The School of Inspired Arts is closed for the holiday but Sid Morris has agreed to give the Frenchwomen a little private instruction. He stands when they come through the door and bows—an admittedly false gesture, but one he's found exceptionally successful when working with women of any age. The two shrug off their coats, commenting on the unseasonable cold and the snow—always snow—this winter. The City paralyzed; sidewalks shoveled willy-nilly; everyone exhausted, has he noticed?

This Simone, of course, the talker. At dinner Sid Morris hardly got a word in edgewise and that was simply to ask for the check. He had heard, among other things, the excruciating details of the late Henry, a man who taught at a private school uptown, one of those brownstones with a crimson door where the boys spilled out every afternoon at 3:30, their white shirttails untucked: boys who wore their privilege as lightly as the clip-on ties now stuffed in their pockets. Henry had taught them mathematics and the art of something he called civil living—how to set oneself according to the rules, and there were rules, the boys were made to understand, thanks to Henry. They were never confused for hooligans, the late Henry would say, no matter the generation, because the generations changed as quickly as the boys did, the late Henry understanding himself to be stalwart at his post, a captain on the bow of a sailing ship, his telescope raised to chart the course far beyond those who teemed and cavorted in the waves below, uncouth, aggressive, snot in their noses, greasy hair.

Simone had said none of this but this is what Sid Morris thought, listening or, better, drifting, thinking of his own upbringing, far away from civil living and the men who understood it. He could picture the charming Henry, a Sunday painter who, Simone said, softly and taking Sid's sleeve, when given the understanding of his impending death, did as his father had done before him: painted bridges. Not the bridges of Paris—it had been years since they lived in that city—but the bridges of New York, beginning with what he called the mighty Washington and then moving from the Verrazano to the Brooklyn.

But you can only do so much with time, she said.

Toward the end, the two had stood somewhere in Chinatown, the crowds of tourists and elderly Chinese pushing at them, bumping into him. The street stank, littered with the remains of some godforsaken parade. All those dead fish packed in ice staring heavenward. Her husband held the box of oils she had given him years ago for his birthday, his skin waxed, unrecognizable. He waved good-bye, heading across Broadway as the light changed—her husband of fifty-eight years, she said.

Fifty-eight years, she said, and there had been a rare pause as Simone withdrew her hand from Sid's arm and the waiter delivered the third round of drinks.

She had been among the lucky, truly—to meet him, to end up here—given the brutalities of war. Did he know the brutalities of war? And to this Sid Morris understood he was to give no answer. He was simply to nod, which he did, as he thought somewhat pretentiously and of no consequence of *Guernica*, of himself in a younger form standing before the painting's heavy gilded frame, in that weak light, sketching in the faraway museum black with oil and smoke and red velvet walls or, possibly, burgundy. Everything comes to pass, Simone said, adding, her voice lowered: Marie did not fare as well. Terrible story, she said. He listened to the terrible story and tried to conjure Marie's face, but he had no clear recollection beyond her eyes, very blue. He preferred Simone's face anyway: the way she painted it just so, the lipstick outlining her lips, cracked, cracking, much of it on the linen napkin in her lap and a bit on her front tooth, slightly crooked and smaller than a front tooth should be, a baby front tooth, yellow, stained from coffee, teas, smeared in red, her eyes, too, outlined in kohl like Cleopatra or the exotic women of a former time.*

---

*And it occurs to Sid Morris, once again, that perhaps women are just depictions of women, representations; women wear *masks,* is the point, slip them on slip them off. Photographs from times past: clunky beads, alabaster or jade, smocks with bold patterns, clip-on earrings—is there anything more delicious? Photographs of women at long tables looking bored or interested—probably always both. Dancers, writers, women who read books—Sappho, de Beauvoir, those kinds of girls—models slipping off Chinese robes before taking their provocative positions on the stool, or the phoenix-winged divans, lion-footed, claw-footed, the talons clutching those wooden balls so tightly they might pop. His thoughts move quickly, alighting in a church in Spain and then settling in a different place, an abandoned barn, upstate New York: a sharp spring cold, a too bright out of winter sun. They'd watched as the wrens built their nests beneath the eaves, the ones with the seed-colored beaks, straw gripped, tiny things, their nests cattywampus, Gretchen had said, a word she knew from where she had come from before, the place she no longer wished to remember. Her skin cold as the air; her hair long and dirty, smelling of the cold air and of more than her and he had felt the cold on her and in a sense the hurry of it all but leaving saw that he had been wrong, again: no one was coming. It was only the two of them; only ever the two of them.

"What?" Sid Morris says, but Simone does not stop talking and besides, he has no idea anyway. She is a woman dressed as a woman framed in black; and he is a man who has had too much to drink, a man who has had too many drinks to count.

"I go on," Simone says, stopping.

"And I grow old," Sid Morris says. He smiles and looks down at the remnants of his dinner, the shrimp tails and asparagus tips he's never much liked the taste of, too squishy. That's right: Henry. They were speaking of the late Henry: how Henry championed boys' theatrics, led the crew team, coached debate. A closet queer? The guy spoke French. Besotted, Simone's word, by the culture. He pictures Cézanne's *L'Estaque* and hears the Ginsberg poem—"In the foreground we see time and life/swept in a race." An interesting color blue, he could tell her. Much to learn from blue, he could say. One of the few colors not found in soil, did she know this? Blue not of the soil but of stone and water, the sea.

The waiter appears to deliver the check. Sid Morris reaches into his suit jacket pocket to Simone's delighted insistence they go "Dutch."

"Quaint," he says, "but no."

He holds Simone's coat, a sleek fur that smells vaguely of mothballs. He imagines she has unfolded it from its usual box for this grand event—dinner with Sid Morris—believing him something better than he is, which is, what? Which would ever be, what?

"Madame," he says, the coat aloft. It makes his arms tired: the evening, the coat, Simone's sharp perfume. The whole thing makes his arms tired.

"Thank you, Mr. Morris," Simone says, slipping in. She stares out from within the mink, or perhaps something smaller and more difficult to skin. "Sidney," she corrects, and suddenly to hear his name, his full name, arrests him, and for a moment Sid Morris believes he might weep as men do, at times, when reminded of their mothers.

"My beauties," Sid Morris says now. "You've ventured into the wilderness."

"We wanted to keep our appointment," Simone says.

"Splendid," he says. The overheated studio is almost unbearable, the radiators knocking as if to explode. Sid's propped the huge filthy studio windows open with crusted paintbrushes, the wind rattling the metal frames, blowing in occasional snow-flakes from the alley that melt the instant they touch the bowed wooden floor. A dance barre runs from here to there; one wall a mirror reflecting the three: two women hunched in boiled wool, a man in suspenders and a dirty shirt, flakes of dry skin on the collar. If the women were to unbutton their blouses and unzip their skirts, unroll their stockings and step out of galoshes and pumps, unhook their brassieres and pull down their panties, they would be near to identical—pale and white, their thin arms and legs veined in blue, their hair sparse, coarse, their breasts flat. If the man were to do the same, they would see that a small sore on his left ankle has turned mean and raw; that his under-pants are yellowed at the crotch, and that he, too, has grown hairless—pale, dark spots blossoming across his chest like mush-rooms after a rainstorm. But as it is, buttoned up, the three look fine, even fit, for this weather, this terrible winter. Simone and Marie shaking out their heavy coats, handing them to the gal-lant Sid, who lays them over the barre as if they are sleeping children. Lighter, the women stand at their easels and begin, again. Somewhere the paint-splattered radio plays—batteries and a dial gone missing though the station never changes, the public one, with the sonorous announcer now droning on about Chopin, always Chopin. Sid asks if they'd like tea; he's on his second pot.

"Late night?" Simone asks.

"Wonderful night," Sid says. "Not late enough." He may wink, or not. Marie doesn't see. She looks at the paintings on the other easels, ignoring. She should have expected this from her friend; it's what Abe always said, the flirt. He suspected her of indiscretions and even, once or twice, of directing her attentions at him although Marie had teased he was only imagining—she's harmless, Marie would say, or she comes by it naturally. Anyway, no matter: this is all from before and here they are, now, standing in the School of Inspired Arts, two old friends and a man they have known for a short time, a renegade, as he himself liked to say, a ne'er-do-well from way back. She listens to the two of them— she can't help it, boisterous Simone!—and then she does not, then she focuses on the other work, on the other easels, metal and wood, canvases stacked along the outer walls, some turned in and others out: the model's hip in a flourish, a detail of her neck and face, the back of her head, her chignon or what had once been called a chignon, parts of the model stacked here and there, worked out in detail, nothing at all, bone and flesh and color, and on others indistinguishable forms, visions from imaginations.

Helen, the art historian, has finished another of the series. She calls it now Life Underwater: here St. Patrick's Cathedral, a homeless man floating up, rising toward the surface, unfurled from his shabby blanket like a figure out of Magritte. This Sid Morris had said the last class or the class before, praising Helen from behind as she added shading to the silhouette beneath the wave's white cap, the homeless man oblivious, laid out like a corpse—she said she saw these things, similar to the visions of the saints. For example, St. Catherine, she said. Religion, magic, she said, and then left it at that, Sid Morris preferring no one ever explained. Besides, words in that room drift like feathers to the filthy floor and are forgotten.*

---

*It would be impossible to articulate her visions anyway. They are the concoctions of a fervent mind, whipped of fondant, nightmares, Helen would say. Her puns, her bad jokes: her ancient history—this series inspired by Debussy's "La Cathédrale Engloutie," and did anyone even remember the tolling of those bells? That sound? Her Debussy now mostly forgotten, like poor Braque behind the giant Picasso. Of her paintings her youngest still says brilliant though she knows her other daughters think odd or, at best, therapeutic, that a word she has come to despise—her habits tallied for their restorative properties rather than for what they are: her life; her spirit.

This scene appeared to her already formed. the river rising, silhouettes black and one-dimensional as photographic plates, exposed on the glass panes of the new condo towers as the water roils below. The silhouettes were as stark as the shadows of Hiroshima victims burned into the sidewalks, she would say. She had witnessed that firsthand, she and Carl visiting the peace museum for an afternoon and here the first inkling of a loosened world. *The* work of history, she argued at the time, a loosened world (she always argued), *the* work of history, she argued: destruction. She argued this with Carl over rice wine in Kyoto, the girls still little, tucked in bed. It was the most beautiful city: the paint store the size of a shoe box she found the first day, the old man inside at his worn wooden desk. The desk and the old man carved from the same tree, she told Carl. The old man said he sewed the brushes by hand and in a black-clay pot ground the pigment from berries and bark and seeds and dirt: the colors she had never seen before or since. An indigo blue you could drink, she told Carl, pouring the last of their rice wine into her tiny cup—that, too; the beauty of that, too, she said to Carl. Look. Look at this, she said, holding up the tiny cup, its shape perfect, fitting like a little bird in the palm of her hand. She remembered. Drunk, she remembered, or near enough, though at the time she had felt simply wise. How, she had said, can we destroy such beauty? How can any of us live with ourselves? But Sid Morris says, never explain.

Duane Reade has painted the model's face, her skull rolled on his canvas like a smooth egg, unbroken, symmetrical, scrubbed of makeup; her skin pinkish, fresh. She is not so old, after all. She is really just a child but it would take a fool not to notice Duane Reade's infatuation. The young man who never speaks has painted a house with a pitched roof beneath a large, bright sun; her favorite. She would like to walk up its simple sidewalk and knock on the door. This is what Sid Morris said as well; he said, I would like to walk up and knock on the door. What would I find? he said, standing behind the young man as the young man, bent as if to break, continued to furiously paint. They had all been listening, pretending they were not.

But the young man who never speaks said nothing.

"How do I look?" Simone is asking. She has moved to the model's couch, the shawl draped over her bare arms. "It's too hot in here."

"Gorgeous," Sid Morris says. "Arch your back a bit," he says.

"I'm going to take a little nap," Simone says. "I'm a sleepy cat," she says.

"You're a beauty," Sid Morris says. "Hold entirely still."

On Monday, Marie will fly to California to visit Jules. She must first finish her universe—the suns and moons, the forest. A present! Marie's menagerie, Sid Morris has called it.

Jules has not invited her, but she has said her old bones could use a little sunshine. She promised not to be in the way.

"I never said you'd be in the way," he said.

"I know," she said.

"You can stay as long as you like," he said.

"I'll stay five days. Five days seems a good number."

"We'll go to La Jolla," he said. "I'll take you to the ocean."

"That would be wonderful," she said.

She will wrap her menagerie in shiny wrapping paper with a big bow. He'll be amazed and think he's back on the stoop in Chelsea, sitting with his father and mother, a young couple with time to spare, their feet on the cool steps, the sun setting a bit too early so it catches them by surprise, the dusk, the long shadows slanting across the seminary, lighting the red brick to a glow. They might hear the bells then; the bells are always ringing.

Walking back from the School of Inspired Arts in the already early dark, Marie and Simone slide their boots along the icy sidewalks like little girls.

"It will ruin your new soles," Simone says. "An outrage."

"They're old boots," Marie says.

"Are they? They look new. Gorgeous," Simone says, linking Marie's arm. The two steady one another over the rubble of salt and sand on the blocks south to the Seventh Avenue crossing—waiting for the ding ding ding of the light that signals to the blind who congregate on the corner of Twenty-Third from the Center for the Blind that they can go. The days are shorter—it is not yet 6:00 and very dark. Stars or perhaps those are satellites shine, faintly, and a narrow moon rends the sky above Chelsea Piers. There, years ago, Marie held Jules's hand as he climbed onto the pony's back; the ring next to the garbage barges and the unused piers and the West Side Highway long gone, the ponies, who knows?

Someone has a fire going—that smell—Marie's street quiet with fresh snow, snow on the two potted evergreens outside the Korean flower shop and crowning the brownstone lions Jules fed as a boy, stuffing their jaws with dried leaves, amazed to find the jaws empty the next day. Those lions have big appetites, she told him. They eat everything all up. Now she scoops the snow crowns off the lions to toss.

Simone does the same then laughs. "Do you think we are ever truly old?" she says. "I mean, inside ourselves, old? Ready to be old?"

# VIII

Margaret Constantine, Dr. Constantine, PhD, in early childhood education from Berkeley and interim head of Progressive K–8, sits by the dim fire watching the Duraflame dissolve to blue: Who We Are due by the end of next month and she should set an example.

She sips her scotch and tries to think, distracted by the photograph of Ariel beaming up from her lap, white-framed, squinting, taken from one of the several cardboard boxes she has yet to unpack, her tenure here short.

She could begin with Thackeray and Dickens, though she prefers Kiran Vicram, the forgotten philosopher, an Indian disciple of Jung rarely if ever read in the West and soon to disappear in the East as well, his books out of print, regrettably but understandably because, Who was he?

She had discovered him by accident, a footnote in the autobiography of H. G. Wells, and why H. G. Wells at all except for her passing undergraduate interest in free love, open marriage, and, admittedly, time travel, interests she grew out of and still, Kiran Vicram remained: a man who sought out Jung with a schizophrenic child, *his* schizophrenic child, Lily, a girl in her late teens who sadly would not survive Jung's treatment, this then a tragedy, *the* tragedy, of the man's long, long life. There is often a tragedy, Margaret has come to understand.

But Kiran Vicram. She had read it; she had read all of it, gathered in more than twenty-three volumes and published posthumously. In fact, Margaret had read so much about Vicram's life she could recite it at random: a hypergraphic, he had filled twenty-three volumes as well as an additional three-volume appendix. Why she sought him out she could not exactly say, only that at particular moments, by either accident or design, persons appear from nowhere to point you in a certain direction. He had pointed her in a certain direction, had ushered a path for her by his very example: perseverance, fortitude, courage, appearing so vivid in print it was as if he rose from the page to meet her mid-sentence, wavy, translucent, warped as old glass but not that, not translucent: thin as onionskin but real somehow and effortlessly beautiful.

In Volume III, still a young boy, brown and waiflike, Vicram stood among a group of similar-looking young boys in the ghastly orphanage in Calcutta, a wet shine in his eyes. He had found himself there, deposited by a destitute and widowed father, and there he stayed, excelling at the missionary school, studying cross-legged in the weak halo cast by the streetlamp outside the orphanage gates.

In IV through VI he disappeared among the cows and the beggars and the ruins of those streets, a runaway like so many of them, homeless, starving, picking through the trash heaps for bits of copper and coal, befriending a darker boy named Bronze, who figured prominently in Volume VII for the character of his conscience and the depth of his soul—some of Vicram's less inspired sentences, true, and yet she felt happy to see Vicram make a friend, to see Vicram and Bronze at a café in Stockholm, the two wearing dark suits with white shirts and ties, looking fresh-shaved and smart, flanked by women.

How they got to Stockholm forms the crux of Volumes V and VI, in chapters gamely titled "Quality of the Brain and Body Concerned," "First Start in Life," and "Struggles." The remaining volumes fascinating reading, though Dr. Constantine had paused for some time, exhausted all over again by Volume XVII, which told the devastating tale of Lily, the ill daughter, and the running attendant losses in Vicram's life, losses something Dr. Constantine knew well: first T. R. Constantine, eclipsed by his wife's success as a graduate student and inclined, even before, toward moodiness, descended into a full-blown depression and left her six weeks into Ariel's babyhood. In a different story, T. R. Constantine may have guaranteed Margaret and Ariel an impoverished, wizened life— but not in hers. Margaret Constantine, soon to be Dr. Constantine, was not made of that metal, she'd been forged by stronger stuff and so, given her depressive husband's abrupt departure and her yowling baby girl, she chose to storm the department head-on and make her mark in the one way available to her: sex. She'd come up with the idea while having drinks with her soon to be thesis adviser at a place in one of the charming towns east of the bay: "So," she had said. "What do you do for fun?"

"Sex," he said, leering.

Behind him some fated fluke bubbled in the tank; above them a net was hung from here to there.

"Oh," she said, lighting a cigarette, ignoring his hand on her thigh.

Her dissertation documented the clear evidence that the notion of an inherent innocence in childhood had no biological precedent per se—in this she drew mainly from the work of Erikson and Ping—and that babydom (*baby-doom*, she wrote) was an outdated sociological construct, along with parental guidelines, movie rating systems, and any other twentieth-century conduit of oversight. The very idea that children needed to be kept innocent (Innocence is Ignorance, she wrote), screened from what adults might view as inappropriate material, was absurd, and, with the obvious encouragement of her adviser, she chose sex as her best weapon. Sex is for All the Young, she wrote, shortening it to SAY Anything. (The stir pleased the department, who went along happily, awarding Margaret Constantine the Katherine Bement Davis Prize for outstanding scholarship, Katherine Bement Davis a long-ago pioneer of something and named one of the three most distinguished women in America at the Panama-Pacific International Exposition of 1915.)

This had all happened in a flurry: in Dr. Constantine's twenties; in the 1970s; in the froth and tumble of the Second Wave stirring up and washing ashore all those rainbow bubbles in its greasy foam, the long, coarse hairs of mermaids tangled around shiny shells that only dulled when dried. There were so many of them! Or us! The trash that accumulated! Difficult to remember what it was all about or, rather, not, but painful given now, with Who We Are more to the point—Dr. Constantine fully aware of the tenor of the times—her general mandate, *the* General Mandate: Identity or, rather, Personhood or, rather, as the educational consultant hired by Progressive K–8 defined it, Self.*

---

*Personhood, he explained, was out due to the Supreme Court muddling of the word, and Identity felt over, too late twentieth century. "Self is streamlined, contemporary, now," the educational consultant said, he formerly of the Clinton, Bush, Obama administrations and once, lifetimes ago, the associate director of the recently defunct National Museum of Tolerance. The simplicity of *self*, he said. "In four letters it somehow references *me* and *sell*."

"And *elf*," Bud Charger, the cutup of the six-member committee elected to draft Progressive's Mandate for the Next Phase, had added.

Still, sometimes that collective of women comes back to Margaret like an old song, a long-ago, welcome chorus: the little one, Connie, who organized—sit-ins, marches, buttons pressed on housewives outside the A&P. Connie danced: Margaret could still see Connie dancing in Vivien's living room. Vivien another one—left by her first husband, the love of her life, a Russian aristocrat she met in Hawaii, military, something: a story. They were all just stories. Pregnant when transferred to California, Vivien couldn't fly and so the aristocrat went alone. *Sayonara, mon amie.* But there were kind men, too; we weren't all women, she'd say. There were men who mimeographed petitions, who brewed coffee, who racked their bearded brains for rap sessions: everyone gone now, taken under just as suddenly by the stormy, turbulent sea.

She had lived in a small white Victorian off People's Park, birds-of-paradise lining the walk, blue glass bottles she collected at flea markets cluttering the windows of her tiled kitchen so that on especially sunny days she felt as if she swam to her whistling teakettle. A stream of men replaced T.R., and then a few women, and then no one, really. She felt no need. Ariel grew up and flew away, ascending through the chimney on a particularly raw and foggy morning in Scotland. She had taken her daughter there to apprehend the monster, a graduation present, Ariel a more natural scholar than herself or T.R., now recovering and slogging it out at a third-tier community college in Rhode Island. He still called from time to time to discuss their salad days, or something of Ariel's he'd read, or the fact of his prostate, which, once removed, had released him to what he took to calling his feline self, softer, more aloof.

So Ariel, then: Ariel is what she has, or had: Ariel with her beautiful mind and lovelier face, Ariel on their last morning in Scotland, a thick sweater rolled at the wrists that dwarfed her thin hands as she pushed a sausage around the plate with a tinny Scottish fork. She said she could "buy" none of it, whatever it was—they were having a disagreement over something Margaret couldn't, or wouldn't, understand. She only knows that on that raw and foggy morning, as she leaned toward Ariel to say, I adore you, she heard the pop. The tiniest of sounds: her daughter dissolved in smoke, swirling with the updraft out of sight.

What If your daughter is lost with the updraft?

The day before, they had hiked to Loch Ness, the monster presumably slumbering in the depths. The bicyclist had stopped and offered to memorialize them ahead, on the famous Anderson stone, the rocky outcrop from which legend had it the monster could best be viewed. The bicyclist read from his guidebook what they already knew, the bicyclist a young man eager to introduce himself as Michael.

Enter Michael. Enter heartbreak. Kiran Vicram would give it an entire volume but Margaret Constantine needs just a few sentences to describe the boy, the thief, the daughter poacher: a tanned young man wearing a thin silver bracelet. She, too, could see his beauty.

His companion had broken his leg and collarbone—struck, actually, by a pickup truck with a load of sheep, weeks ago. Yeah, sheep, he said. He had continued the trip alone and now couldn't help himself, seeing such a pretty girl and her pretty sister. (Hah! Margaret did not say.)

Fat gray clouds edged a weak sun, the weather a rainy constant, stone cold. At night she and Ariel pulled itchy blankets to their chins and closed their eyes, exhausted. Mrs. MacIntyre insisted they take the hot-water bottles up; she of the Glasgow collector MacIntyres, found through Rachel's guides as they had found everyone. Coins. Silver spoons. A cousin in Leeds fancied

letters of the American presidents: Hamilton, too. Mrs. MacIntyre
had made her own mark with dolls, nineteenth-century, porcelain, they'd see a few on the Mother Hubbard in the hall: Lucy
and Faith, her favorites. Sisters. Don't touch, they'll wear away,
Mrs. MacIntyre said.

Michael, Michael says, reaching out to shake her hand first
and then Ariel's—the silver bracelet!—balancing his bicycle
against his bony hip.

Your poor friend—this from Ariel—is he all right?

He wanted to quit anyway.

I'm sorry.

I think he secretly missed his girlfriend.

You? Ariel asks. (She has completely forgotten her.)

I'm a loner, essentially

(Essentially? thinks Margaret. *Essentially?*)

Oh, says Ariel.

He was lucky, Michael says. He *should* have been killed.
The trucker didn't even see him. "Stopped and asked after the
satchel in the road. Didn't even know he'd hit a guy."

"Jesus!" (This from Ariel.)

"I'll give the Scottish cops their chops. They were on it in an
instant and took him to this little hospital—"

"Where?"

"Dunberry. Beautiful town. I'll show you if you'd like. Somebody's from there. Robert Burns or the guy who married Elizabeth Taylor—"

"Burton."

"Right. Robert Burton. Anyway, it's this little hospital run by
nuns and there's like three other patients and this freakin' *priest*
runs up and I'm thinking he's so bad they're giving him his last
rites—"

"Oh my God."

"And I don't want to interrupt to say he's *Jewish* because what the hell do I know? Maybe it works on everybody and so I'm standing there thinking. I don't know what I was thinking. I was just standing there. But the priest is the doctor."

"What?"

"I know, right? Like that joke the father's the doctor only the joke is the mother's the doctor—"

"Right!" (Ariel laughing.)

"And then he's in surgery and I'm just there and then I start thinking how we left his bicycle—what was left of it—wherever we were and so I go and it's the truck driver with his load of sheep. He's been waiting the whole time."

"Wow."

"I love these people."

"I know what you mean."

"You do?"

"Totally."

And so on: Soon they exhaust Scotland and its people and are on to Cornell, Duke, MIT, Yale. Between the two they know the entire world. Margaret listens and then she does not. Then she pages Rachel's guides: *West from the Anderson Stone, locate the cross where the Scottish hero McIntry fell on his sword in King Arthur's time, if the Welsh monk Nennius is to be believed. Look for the trampled grass, the evidence of pilgrimage, the occasional blunt stub of the candle and Mardi Gras beads given the recent popularity of Medieval and Celtic gatherings.*

She thinks to share what Rachel says with Ariel now, even with Michael, but the hitch in Ariel's voice gives everything away. She follows the two toward the Anderson stone, where Michael, predictably, insists: a shot of Margaret and Ariel, together. He's beyond the frame already. Here, too, in the photo as Ariel looks up from her mother's lap, shading her eyes.

A tractor startles the crows that caw and lift toward the gray clouds. Somewhere always a rainbow, Michael informs them, another thing about Scotland the constancy of good luck, and also, the heather, larkspur, and yarrow.

From over the ridge the German walkers approach with a blast of German. They have hiked from Inverness and won't stop until they reach the sea.

This all and what else; that in the morning she will say whatever she says to make it not right; she will say whatever she says to make Ariel disappear. New Zealand of all places, an acre of garden in back, gargantuan trees, a raggedy dog adopted in Auckland. Michael is out of the picture. Ariel is finishing another book. This from T.R.—who wouldn't know a thing but for the fact of his absent prostate; "I make it my business to never hang up without saying I love you," he told Margaret, as if this were a revelation. And then, hanging up, he said, "I love you."

# IX

On an earlier Thursday, Sid Morris circled the class during Friendly Break, his cigarette sharp. If they were to turn off the lights and blacken the windows they would see only the orange glow of its embers as Sid Morris sucks in and breathes out, exhaling smoke. Smokers evolutionary dragons, Helen once said to the two old newcomers; Olympians evolutionary mermaids. Helen's round glasses are framed in thick plastic, black as her dyed hair. (A cheaper brand, Simone said. The way Helen peered through the lenses as if trying to see in murky water, her eyes exaggerated and a little off, Simone thought— she's been through something; and did Marie notice how certain times she went so close to her canvas it seemed she might be smelling it? And other times she squeezed her eyes shut like she was trying to paint in the dark?)

One hundred years ago today, Sid Morris said.

Cézanne said, he said.

*Nota bene*, he said.

He blew the last of his smoke toward the windows though the windows were still painted shut so the smoke lilted and sank like a day-old balloon.

"Painting is not copying . . . it is *realizing* one's sensations."

The boy who does not speak raised his hand but Sid Morris did not notice.*

"Cézanne's principle of certainty," Sid Morris continued, "which is bullshit, no? So maybe it's the translation. Sensations have nothing to do with certainty, more incertainty."

"Uncertainty," Helen corrected.

"You certain?" Sid Morris said, dropping his spent cigarette into the coffee can that holds down one of the corners of the cheap Chinese-factory-ed print of Cézanne's knives and onion and apples scattered across Cézanne's famously raked table; a half-empty Dunkin' Donuts box, courtesy of Duane Reade, holding down the other.

Helen nods, blinking. "Yes," she says.

"The point is," Sid Morris says. "This. Now. Paint on your brush, wind at your back, my crappy studio. This is the only certainty. Here: your sensations; your body existing for its moment in time. Everything else is crap."

In the corner, the tattooed model almost dozing on the pile of their soft winter coats lets out a small snort and shifts her position to fetal. Then silence. Snow, again. Tiny flakes like spewed ash swirl through the alley, the air shaft, ticking the filthy windows that later someone, unable to bear the dry heat any longer, chisels open. And from below a burst of laughter seems to set off a raucous scuffle, as if the waitstaff at the Chinese restaurant were chasing a greased pig.

At this Helen stands from her uncomfortable stool, her hand on the back of her canvas as if steadying a nervous companion. She wears a floral tunic, and beads she bought years ago at the

---

*What you would find in my house is Mom and Dad sleeping it off upstairs and the rest of us crowded around the television beneath the dog blanket.

old flea market on Sixth and Twenty-First, the amber ones that, if you hold them to the light, set the world in sepia, back a century or two.

"He looked for a new system of representation. Realism was bankrupt, he said—the still life as dead as the pheasants in the composition. He wanted to paint only the impressions of what he saw: light, space, color."

"My point," Sid Morris says.

The Thursday group, perhaps inspired by Helen, the art historian, the way she remains standing, blinking, fingering the thick beads around her neck, her floral tunic oddly perfect with the model's Renaissance scarf and Sid Morris's beret, as if the all of them, combined, are something out of a lost Vuillard, join her to form a circle around Cézanne's table. They study the cheap reproduction, considering, and when they return to their collective canvases, they vow to do better.

"Thank you for leading us to our sensations," Simone says, smiling at Sid Morris.

"And delivering us from evil," Duane Reade adds, his thin, new mustache, later admired by the prostitute he regularly visits above the one-dollar-slice pizza on Thirty-Seventh and Tenth, dusted with powdery white sugar.

X

Marie sits in the lush garden, a place that still amazes her: lime trees and lemon trees and orange trees and even a grapefruit tree, though its grapefruits are the size of lemons. There is a small statue of Buddha on a lotus, water trickling over his round, greened belly; the sound is the sound of water. The smell is the smell of eucalyptus. The home is the home of Jules's new partner, Larry.

"Oh," she had said.

She sits in the lush garden watching Larry decorate the fruit trees for a party, stringing colored lights and tinsel. In her honor, Jules has told her. They have invited their set.

The wanderings of her vivid imagination stay on the mantel—Larry preferring not to tack the wall: he isn't into nails and wires, he says, but he's delighted to keep it there behind his collection of vintage glass.*

---

*She will take it back, she's decided—its suns and moons and forest thick with spruce and what you cannot see, what's hidden there—when she returns. She will sneak it into her suitcase and carry it to New York and if Jules asks she'll tell him there is more to do, that it is a work in progress.

The call is for her, Jules says. He stands with the telephone in his hand, a look on his face, then moves to where Larry hangs the lights, near the roses where a few weeks back Larry released a bag of ladybugs to eat the aphids, ladybugs she has picked from her clothing since she arrived, counting their spots just for fun, announcing their age. Jules is saying something to Larry, leaning into Larry, as she listens to Simone's Katherine.

"I don't know how to tell you," Katherine's begun, words Marie hears and quickly buries.

Simone!

A taxi at the dangerous crossing at Ninth and Twenty-Third—so close to her mother's apartment and she'd always warned—a crowd, some Samaritan fashioning a blanket from a coat then something else; the ambulance arrived within minutes too late. Marie listens and then she does not. Then she watches as her son and his partner lean into one another in the sunlight, watches as the two of them—in an instant—disappear. Abe used to do that walking home: disappear. She waited for him on the stoop, waited for him to turn the corner and put his hand up. Remember how he put his hand up? Waving? A happy man, Mother had said—this to Sylvie or perhaps Rose, the two fingertip curls and an occasional lipstick—be sure to marry a happy man.

They had bought the house in Chelsea for a song; they were pilgrims, adventurers. Look, look! Abe had said: the Monticello banister hewn from a single tree, chiseled smooth pumpkin wood—extinct!—and shipped all the way from the Carolinas, the planks as wide as the beams for the king's mast. Look! Look! Abe had said. Now soon he will turn the corner and she is waiting, waiting, watching for his wave, his smile. The light may very well swallow him whole. She grips the thick limb in anticipation, the cold bark on her palms, the tree alive with bees. Beneath her, blackened fruit litters the ground. Apricots. She could break her back but still she strains to see against the sunset glare reflected in the polished windows of St. Claire's Rectory. Soon Abe will be home, she knows. Soon. She has been waiting here forever, she will tell him; she was feeling all alone.

# XI

Elizabeth recognizes the dark-haired woman from block patrol taping something up in the hallway outside Dr. Constantine's office. "Oh," Elizabeth says. "You did it."

"What?" the woman says.

"Who We Are," Elizabeth says, pointing.

"We're all somebody," the woman says, which reminds Elizabeth of that Dickinson poem. She thinks to make a joke and say, *I'm nobody, who are you?* but the dark-haired woman seems in a hurry, smoothing tape on the photograph of her family as if trying to make it stick: two young children, one of them much fairer than the other, stand in front of a Ferris wheel at dusk. Behind them stretches a long horizon, pink at the edge, beautiful. She would like to read it but that feels wrong, like sneaking a peek at a diary left out on a bedside table. She shouldn't be too interested—she doesn't know why she is so interested but she finds the stories fascinating: rappelling down cliff walls, sailing the Atlantic: women and women, men and men, single women, exotic places, colors, family pets—who knew?

Does everyone else have a composed life? Is everyone else sure of how things should be? The choices they've made?

Why do I always question? she asks Slotnik on one of her regular Wednesday sessions, to which Slotnik, predictably, says, I don't know, why?

"Have you written yours?" the woman asks.

"Writer's block," Elizabeth says.

"I hear you," the woman says, walking away.


"They met at the top of a Ferris wheel," Elizabeth's saying. She's on a date with Pete, the Vietnamese place. "So naturally, that's where he proposed. They were both doing fieldwork in Central America and decided to combine forces. Or that's what she wrote. It's amazing. They've opened some kind of school there for the indigenous. They're only there, or here, half the year, hence her disappearance after block patrol."

"That doesn't make sense," Pete says. He's wearing one of his old frayed button-downs and the lights are dim, candle-lighted lights. She remembers how nice it is to be with him in a crowded place—she might lean against him later, they might walk arm in arm. Within the restaurant bamboo shadows are cast on the screens that line the walls in elaborate illumination; every once in a while a parrot, or some such bird, shrieks as if chased by a parrot-eating monkey.

"I know it doesn't make sense," she says. "It's got to be totally exhausting, here to there, there to here. I mean one day we're patrolling Bleecker for pedophiles and the next day, poof, she's gone."

"No, no, I mean meeting on top of a Ferris wheel. How would you meet on top of a Ferris wheel? You're either in the same carriage or not, and if you're not, then you wouldn't be shouting across the void."

"Well, maybe they did. Maybe they shouted across the void,"

Elizabeth says. "What's wrong with shouting across the void?" She wraps her vegetable roll in a lettuce leaf, or frond—it's huge—and takes a bite, spilling most of it.

"I smell a rat," Pete says. He crunches and chews.

"Central America, too?" she says.

"A pack of lies," he says, pressing his folded napkin to his lips, smiling. "A Who We Are fantasy."


Later, they walk the bike path home, the new Chelsea pulsing, the High Line a rising, parallel path, too crowded on a night as balmy as this one to maneuver. Elizabeth leans on Pete and links his arm, smelling the wool smell of his coat against the briny Hudson, the smell she's always loved. He bought the coat years ago in a thrift shop in Paris, in an arrondissement of a higher number not known for anything in particular—they were lost, actually, had gotten out at the wrong Métro, the coat right there, a dusty gray hanging on a long sidewalk rack of old wool coats. For a while Pete said he felt sure his new coat had been worn by a member of the Résistance, not an important member, but a member nonetheless, a smallish guy, maybe, like him, a guy who mostly assisted the others, rolling cigarettes, running messages, humping pots and pans and supplies for the meager meals he and his comrades would eke out in the woods, his wool coat his one good thing until, maybe, he was caught and killed. Most of them were, Pete said. The Germans executed all the men of the closest town when their munitions trains were attacked—like the famous one, Les Vroon, near the Boulogne woods. Maybe he had been part of that operation, left his wool coat and his comrades in the woods, Pete said. This, in May, the war almost won. He might have been part of that, the coat presented to his mother by his comrades, the coat along with the change in its pockets, a few francs, a saint's medal from his first communion; an empty coat for a boy.

"Wow," Elizabeth had said hearing Pete's made-up story. "I guess maybe," she had said, and then, for the rest of the evening or at least until they returned to their hotel, a crappy walk-up in the Sixteenth, she had called him amour, Pierre.

Across the street the brownstone windows look dark. Inside Ben watches television or sits in front of a computer screen, newly thirteen and allowed to stay home alone. Still. There's a sudden secrecy to her boy. She imagines scaling the brick around back or shimmying the mulberry next door to where she might peer in through their kitchen window and see.

What If he's no longer there?

What If he's disappeared?*

A shallow light leaks from Marie's garden-floor windows. She doesn't sleep much, Marie. Sometimes Elizabeth hears her hobbling around downstairs, late at night. They are both awake, owner and renter, and why not? The neighborhood's suddenly too loud, sirens and helicopters and the frenzied revelers packed on the sidewalks, in the bars, the restaurants. The electronic

---

*Ben *has* disappeared. He is no longer Ben, his body turned inside out, wrong. The ugly part of him out though he doesn't give a shit about that because what he mostly gives a shit about is his dick. It's like an itchy sweater. That's how it is now for Ben, Ben would say, if he ever had the nerve to answer Ms. Kim, the incredibly hot ethics teacher's question of How is it for you? How is it for me? I don't understand French for shit. The coach thinks I suck. How is it for you, Ms. Kim? Or his mother's: the way she opens the door and stands in the doorway of his room, looking. "What's up?" she'll say but it's *rhetorical* because she just stands there looking like she can't quite figure out where she is even when he says bye-bye, or get out, or yells to next time knock, looking like there's something she's trying really hard to see and it isn't him, or isn't who he is, or was.

pulse everywhere: on the new screens on top of taxis and over subway entrances, on the bigger screens that dwarf the skyline, encircle the buildings, the skyscrapers; the one on Macy's like Orion's belt—a constellation of flashing explosions, crashing automobiles, detonating bridges. The male actors hold guns the size of Mack trucks and the women, their nipples taut in bikini tops or push-up bras, smile out into the chaos as if looking for a good fuck. Someone has tilted the globe and everything's rushing in, or down, wrenched from the hand.

"I'm going to stay here for a while," she calls to Pete, sitting on the stoop. "Just a minute," she says.*

"Elizabeth?" Pete says. He is inside, just beyond the front door, waiting; he must not have heard. "You coming up?" he says.

"Hamster trance," Elizabeth says. "Sorry," she says. She climbs the stoop to where Pete waits and holds out her arms.

"Carry me," she says.

---

*As a little girl, she would fall asleep in her mother's lap on drives home from adult parties, parties where she had been sequestered in the basement rec room with the older kids, a hodgepodge of blemishes and hairstyles arguing over a Foosball point. She sat by herself on the mildewed sofa, a book in her hand, something advanced and a little shady, *Love Story* or *Black Like Me*. She was waiting for the adults to be finished, waiting for the moment to go home, again. In the car her father smoked his pipe; her mother smoked her cigarette, her mother's hand absentmindedly stroking her hair until the eventual bump and stop in the driveway. Then she could open her eyes and sit up to see her father raising the garage door in the headlights, or she could keep her eyes shut, still pretending to sleep, her breathing timed to her mother's hand.

# XII

It starts early, the day. Marie brews tea and watches Roscoe stalk a squirrel. She has put out the bird feeder for the mourning doves and nuthatches but the squirrels are hungry, too; the ground newly thawed, wet. In another landscape, a line of spruce in the distance would appear an inkblot, a punctuation to the endless gray sentence of the morning, but here, on her shortened horizon, only their small back garden: its color in the promise of perennials—daffodils and tulips, the espaliered rose against the back brick wall, the privets in their clay urns wrapped in butcher's paper, hidden still in the dark of the basement to winter. She should bring them up.

There are always things to do: vegetables from the Twenty-Third Street vendor—something dark and leafy, red-veined, to go with the sole or skinless chicken she'll broil for her dinner. She doesn't know the vendor's name, but his face is familiar. She prefers to pick her own, she tells him, approaching with her string bag. She does not imagine he recalls her daily request. He nods as if he doesn't. She would guess him to be Mohammad or Raz. He does not look at her. When she has chosen, he counts her change, his fingers inked and raw with morning cold. Then to the butcher around the corner on Ninth.

But first, tea, her habit, in one of the cups Abe's relatives collected, always on the prowl for what they could, according to Abe, figuratively steal. His great-aunt Eleanor, of the Philadelphia-Greenwich set, best for the bargains—nose like a beagle; stout of frame. Eleanor had bargained for their wedding present, the dragon-spouted teapot worth thousands and the cups to match, gold-leafed, scaly. Sugar bowl, too, even more valuable given its coloring and the quality of the porcelain. Marie pictures the set in the Antoinette cabinet in the foyer, higher than she can reach but still. The foyer! How Abe loved that word. Left the mail in the foyer, he would call. Keys in the cloisonné bowl, foyer! She walks from the back, the yellow kitchen, to the front foyer, blue. French blue. Dark now, sconces of the faux gas variety, unlit, elaborate, brass, fussy. Something Very Grand would find fitting if she looked from her gilded frame. Very Grand rights her hair, her gown, pulls the wrap round her brittle, regal shoulders, military-straight from years of ballet. And so, Marie, she says— she's learned their names!—time goes by, does it not?

Marie finds the stepladder at the mouth of the basement stairs, there for when the gas or electric man comes to read the meter. Foolish, she thinks, before she climbs, but she can almost reach. She just needs a little height, the dragon-spouted teapot long ago stashed on the highest shelf—she hasn't thought of it in years!—a gift from Great-Aunt Eleanor, unable to make the wedding for a buying trip to Leningrad.* The teapot arrived

---

*Letters and diaries were to be had for a song, the whole place in turmoil— Communists, Trotskyites, Nazis: a lost Chekhov, the notebooks of Gogol or, maybe, Pushkin. Great-Aunt Eleanor couldn't wait: she had developed a love of ephemera in old age, of saving that which could not be counted on

weeks after the ceremony wrapped in tea towels in a blue Tiffany box. The box Marie saved for years; the tea towels finally stripped to rags.

Very clever, Abe had said, unwrapping. Clever Eleanor. It even looks a bit like her. "I'm a little teapot, short and stout," he sang. The spout a dragon's head, or something similarly mythological, the handle its tail, puckered with scales: a scaly teapot. The entire thing glazed gold. Odd. Unique. Valuable. For a while, on Brooklyn Sunday mornings, when Marie and Abe were childless and young, they would wake and make love, Abe slipping off her nightgown as she slept, or almost slept. She pretended to be sleeping and then she helped him by taking off her panties, his boxers. They were naked beneath the covers and she was both warm and cold as Abe went under to lick her toes, her legs. She pulled the covers up—could he breathe? Her eyes burned, squeezed tight. She arched her back, twisted. She could still remember.

They stayed in bed drinking tea from the dragon pot, the newspaper spread around them, the sun streaming in. Abe called it a dragon encounter, insisting served this way there was luck involved, a difference in the way the tea tasted.

Marie steps on the stepladder a bit shaky. She's in her nightgown and robe, thin, her face in pots and brushes on the bathroom vanity, eyesight dim, glasses in the pocket of the robe, forgotten, feet slippered, slippery, so that the eventual slip seems almost a question of semantics. That she catches her fall on the corner of the cabinet saves her hip but not her ankle,

---

lasting forever. She pawed through attics, wooden chests, string-wrapped bundles stashed beneath loose floorboards. Wasn't everything worth something? Every sentence? Every sound? She unfolds another square of brittle, inked paper. A confetti of words rains down.

which turns in a way unnatural, fracturing the bone, a tiny jag so painful she cries out, setting off the movie star's twins, newly born and sequestered in the renovated maid's room on the other side of the wall. Their cries mask Marie's own, so that it's a good while later before she's discovered by Sid Morris, who has tracked down Marie's address from the registration form Simone filled in for both of them months ago, and at least one lifetime.

It is Sid Morris who peers through one of the wavy glass panels beside the old oak front door, its brass knocker decidedly beside the point, his eyes adjusting to the dark foyer, the furnishings. He heard the news and has come around, assuming a service of some sort or another, a way to pay his respects to Simone. It is the least he can do, given their dinner out, that time in Madison Square Park, and so on, and so it is Sid Morris who eventually makes out the form of Marie on the floor, the toppled stepladder beside her. It doesn't take much to put two and two together. Jesus Christ, his first thought, believing Marie dead and this an unfortunate and perhaps too complicating association, though his conscience, sharpened by age and his lousy performance with Veritas, leads him to the hardware store on Tenth, the locksmith, the police, the rescue, Marie not dead at all, perfectly healthy, she insists, just resting or perhaps she even dozed off. She refuses the ambulance and asks only for the support of the handsome policeman.

"You looked dead," Sid Morris says.

"I couldn't get up," Marie says.

"It's an orthopedic issue," the policeman says. "There's a clinic on Seventh in the Twenties, can you get there?"

"I'll get her there," Sid Morris says.

"Are you her husband?" the policeman says.

Marie, propped now on the Queen Anne chair upholstered

in maroon velvet, her foot raised, her ankle packed in ice from the Korean deli (she never remembers to fill her trays), is too surprised by Sid Morris's yes to say no.

"Good then," the policeman says. He tears off a form he drops in the cloisonné bowl and it is only then, watching the handsome policeman let himself out, that Marie notices the shards of teapot on the foyer floor, the dragon head miraculously intact, severed as if by guillotine from its magic spout.

# XIII

It is quite late when Elizabeth finds her way into Progressive K–8, the hallway lights out, the classroom lights out, the only glow a watery blue fluorescence from the science room aquarium. She talked the keys out of Bernice Stilton, school secretary, on a separate pretext—Ben's history textbook left beneath his desk and, given his struggles with hypergrandia and so on.*

She promises to return the keys quick as a flash.

Bernice Stilton has understood as she will always understand, the keys clammy with understanding as she passes them over to Elizabeth. "Safe travels," she says; it is cold and her breath comes

---

*The *and so on* is a long list, hypergrandia often one in a constellation of learning challenges formerly known as learning differences formerly known as learning disabilities that have dogged Ben for years, resulting in Elizabeth's purchases of the vitamins B, G, Y, and R3, her consultation with a hypnotist and psychic, and her bedside table loaded with books on various theories and diagnoses. Although Progressive K–8's submandate to Partner with the Parent and its attendant Circle Rap sessions have keyed her in to the epidemic nature of *and so on,* in her heart of hearts she believes most of it only fashion. Such as melancholia; or hysteria.

out in clouds. She stands at the front door to the Penn South building, where she has lived since coming to the City. Rudy Stilton, she
would say, by way of explanation. Then, the rest of life: petitioning
for Adlai Stevenson, John F. Kennedy, his handsome brother, his
poor son. Once, years ago, she stood on the roof of Rockefeller
Center dropping dandelions on the passersby. Once she rolled in
sweats in a chain of women through Sheep Meadow, Central Park,
stopping the bulldozers who were there to bulldoze something she
can't now remember what.

She pulls her robe across her thin chest: Bernice very thin,
and myopic: she squints. She has worked at Progressive for
nearly forty years and almost half as many administrations, the
first the actual grandson of William Winifred Scott, its philosopher founder.*

On her relationship with Dr. Constantine she prefers not to
comment, and it is for this reason that Elizabeth prefaced her
phone call by admitting she knew this was against school policy,
but given the *fickle nature of the changing guard* she hoped Bernice

---

*Winifred after his mother, she the Winifred Scott of the Cooperstown Tran-
scendentalists, a woman so legendary for her ability to detect portals to the
spirit world she counted Mary Todd Lincoln among her high-paying clients,
although Lincoln's desperation to reach her son also led her to every quack
operating along the north-south corridor and finally to a room at Bellevue
Place sanitarium. But everyone agreed Winifred Scott was the real McCoy.
She stood on the steps of the abandoned Home for Destitute Women her
son had found in bankruptcy on Bleecker Street, his dream of an elemen-
tary school grounded on the principles of Locke, Rousseau, and everyone
else he had read in graduate school almost realized but for the portal his
mother divined inside. She urged the spirits to cross back and sealed it as
best she could but warned that given the disasters of the coming centuries,
disasters she saw in blurry detail out of the corners of her eyes, the portal
could open again, and would.

might make an exception. This was close to an emergency, she said. This once. Just tonight. She would return the keys first thing, she promised.

"All right," Bernice had said without a fight.

"I'll be quick," Elizabeth said. "I'll keep the lights out."

"All right," Bernice had said.

It is Bernice's job each morning to raise the flags that hang on the flagpole—U.S. and UN—and to unlock Progressive K–8's large glass doors and prop them open so the children don't get swatted as the busy parents race in and out. It is also Bernice's job to make the coffee in the principal's office, to pull the blinds in the science lab, and to check to make sure the reptiles are still alive—no one eager to repeat the unfortunate Trisi Watkins incident. It is Bernice's job to outfit the volunteer crossing guards and the volunteer morning greeters and to make sure that the cluster of mothers, the Early Birders, whose 7:00 A.M. Steps! class is now up to twenty-five rotations of the four flights leading to Progressive K–8's playground roof, know to move it along for the hordes who will descend at 8:30. It is perhaps for this reason and despite Elizabeth's claim that she'll drop the keys back off by 6:30 that Bernice keeps watch as Elizabeth moves into the Ninth Avenue traffic, steering her bicycle down one of the new bicycle lanes, the light on her helmet flashing as if Elizabeth were her own ambulance on her way to her own emergency.

But Bernice was once a mother, too, and always a working girl, a professional. She drank gin. On weekends she took a pottery course at the New School. In 1963, at a glamorous club somewhere midtown, Frank Sinatra had asked her to dance.

Charmed, she had said.

Why Bernice remembers Frank Sinatra while watching Elizabeth's flashing bicycle light disappear into the stream of Ninth Avenue, taxis piling up here and there and delivery boys hell-bent for somewhere sideswiping one another, she could not say, but returning she feels already regretful, a bit undone by the look of it all, or more specific: Elizabeth Fanning lost in traffic. She wonders if she has done the right thing and knows she has not.

Face the music! Rudy used to say. No one wants to face the music! She can see him now, Rudy. Like Fiorello La Guardia, a real firecracker, a spark plug, a pistol. He gave her a tough time sometimes—he couldn't help it, his own father and so on. You have to consider the tree before you call me a rotten apple, he'd say.

# XIV

A grainy rescue, difficult to see; Sid Morris says Bangladesh or somewhere similarly brokenhearted but Marie thinks Zimbabwe. Surely Africa. Years ago, in the war, men went there to die, Marie says, or to escape, or, she supposed, to win. As far as she could tell they simply pushed one another back and forth across a vast desert. Never mind. She does not know what she is saying: the painkillers.

"What I said," Sid says, chewing. "Brokenhearted."

They sit side by side at Marie's kitchen table eating the quiche Marie made yesterday with the intention of a week of meals and here hardly a crumb left in the pie tin, Sid Morris ravenous. In front of them the television looms—a companion half their age, black and white, cracked, a twisted wire hanger antennaed to the left, drooping though better askew. Sid takes enormous, rude bites, the linen napkin Marie provided tucked into his collared shirt like a lobster bib. The people on the screen fade in and out, disintegrating, reappearing: a crowd jostling and pushing their way onto a boat only slightly less shaky than the boat they're already on; it's a turbulent, black-and-white sea. A few slip and bob in the waves—who is there to save them?

Confusion, a lot of shouting, and then the fallen are pulled back in with great, thick ropes.

"I haven't seen static in years," Sid says.

"I only get PBS," Marie says. "Also something called New York One."

"I know that," Sid says. "The old mayors are always on. Giuliani, the pit bull. Never trusted him. My favorite was always Koch. No bullshit. Or just bullshit. Same difference."

"I watch the *NewsHour*," Marie says. "More?"

"Thank you," Sid says. He holds out his glass and Marie pours. A cheerful white, she called it when he asked its origin, from not so cheerful France.

"France!" Sid had said, as if he had only just thought of it. Tell me, he says. She feels loopy, light; her ankle throbbing. There must be more to the story, he says.

She is too fuzzy-brained, she says. Besides, how could she begin? In the end, it takes only one to die but many to be saved, she says. You did what you had to do. You didn't ask questions.

Understood, Sid Morris says.

She met her husband in Rochester—that's him, there, she says: Abe among Abes and Juleses and Maries, the youngest Abe in his wedding suit, sleeves too short, pants too short, standing in the garden of a family friend.

The gardens Marie could still remember: the peach and magnolia, the lilies of the valley. But Rochester. Yes, Rochester. Brought over by a second cousin eventually. She met Abe there, in Rochester. Abe her late husband, the American, named for the president.

"Deadly," Sid Morris says, putting down his empty glass.

"America?"

"Rochester," he says.

"You've been?" she asks.

"God, no," he says.

She drains her glass, her ankle throbbing. "And you?" she says, changing the subject.

The boys on the street played Ringo-Ringo and stick hockey and the walleyed Eamon, the Irish kid, got a broken jaw from always looking the wrong direction. Those days a lot of cross-eyeds, he says. Not like now.

Italians. Irish. The Jews were there already but they came to his neighborhood later. He tells the joke about the Rabbi and the woman from Miami Beach. He says his first and only wife, Gretchen, overdosed on horse in 1967, but he gets the year wrong. Nineteen sixty-seven the year of his daughter's birth, a year his wife was mostly stoned until she wasn't, pregnant, so pretty the downtown photographer, the famous one, asked to photograph her in the nude, him standing, Sid Morris could still remember, with his hard-on in his leather pants though later Sid heard he mostly preferred boys, Gretchen on the bed in that place where he lived and worked, charcoal on the walls, a message of some sort, words scrambled in a pattern he didn't recognize though one, *veritas*, he liked the sound of, *veritas*, and so asked Gretchen if she had seen but she said no, she had blissed out on being adored, she said. I was adored. Gretchen a nice girl from Ohio—*why, oh why, oh why, oh*—with hair to her hips, white blond, blissed out on being adored. But the boys would not leave her alone and so she shaved her head and bought a bus ticket east. She found her way downtown and picked a pocket or two and so on, and by the time he found her she'd stitched love with red thread on her palm so infected he had to carry her to St. Vincent's.

Poor St. Vincent's! Marie says. She could still picture Abe flirting with the nurses from his double room with the yellow plastic curtain; picture how she sat in the metal chair and wished him out, staring over the rooftops of the Village to a sunset on the Hudson she described to him in detail, the hearing, the old nurse said in the end, the last to go. The old nurse peeled a grapefruit and offered her a segment. She stared out the window, too. Mount Sinai, the old nurse said, has a special floor, five thousand dollars a day, like a four-star hotel, she said. She'd heard but never been, thank God. Movie stars and politicians, kings who could afford to fly in to die on expensive sheets, can you imagine? the old nurse said, juice on her chin she wiped with dry, chapped hands. She had been from one of the islands—Antigua, Anguilla.

I cannot imagine, Marie had said.

Gretchen always thought it still looked a little like love, Sid Morris is saying, I mean, after the scar healed, hardened a purple red. Doesn't it look a little like love? she would say, stoned. Just a little? Then the time she left Veritas in her stroller on Avenue B at midnight, corner of Tompkins Square when Tompkins Square was Tompkins Square, remember?

Sid Morris apologizes for saying too much. It has been a day to let the cat out of the bag, as his mother would have said, his mother what he liked to call an idiom savant.

Streams of black-and-white women and children disembark from a shaky bus, joyful. Many carry animals. Others appear shell-shocked. Now a group of women do a complicated dance involving hand clapping and what looks like singing. "I wonder what they're saying," Marie says.

Sid reaches out his glass, which Marie quickly refills. He has wiped his plate clean. "Have you always had this problem with the picture?" he asks.

"You get used to it," Marie says, watching.

"Do you?"

"My son thinks it's a liability. 'What if there were an emergency?' he says. 'You need a working television,' he says. 'For news,' he says. 'Why?' I say. 'What difference would it make?'"

"I would have appreciated a little static with the mayors," Sid says.

"My son is always talking emergencies," Marie says.

"Like today," Sid says. "Today was an emergency."

Three hours at the doc-in-a-box, a taxi ride to the far East Side, X-rays, strangers—the woman who took her information at radiology strikingly similar to the woman who took her information at geriatrics, and orthopedics, the woman's fingernails to here, striped, dotted with tiny jewels, diamonds? Marie forgot what she was saying, distracted by the nails. She wanted to ask for a scratch. I itch all over, she might have told the woman. Dry skin. Terrible. You turn to dust before you turn to dust. She remembers Simone's hands though that isn't fair. Where is Simone in all this? What has she become? Her cosmetics in a line on her vanity Katherine saying she should toss but her mother would probably come back and rattle her chains.*

"What?" Marie had said.

"Medicare?" the woman said. "Address?" the woman said. "Nice neighborhood," the woman said. "The High Line."

"Yes," Marie said, though she had never been. She had heard

---

*Katherine had given a fine eulogy for her mother. The best she could. Toward the end of it, her voice cracked and her husband had to finish reading, something about elegance in the face of hardship Marie had a hard time following, much less believing, since Simone's hardship had been fairly brief and for the most part she lived a pampered life, a thought Marie immediately banished from her mind, focusing instead on the enlarged photograph Katherine had set on top of Simone's coffin, closed, oddly enough, as Marie was fairly sure that Simone would have loved everyone having a last look, Simone buried in her favorite dress—a green silk the same cut and shade of the one she was discovered in all those years ago by Henry, who took it upon himself to have another made for her fiftieth birthday, a bash at which a drunken Abe had revealed Simone's flirtations.

they were having trouble with an exhibitionist—this from the movie star, quite instrumental, apparently, in its creation.

I won't say exactly, he had said of the exhibitionist's antics, but it's really creepy.

"More?" Sid Morris asks. It's a complicated question, given the trajectory of the conversation, the empty bottle before her.

"In the fridge," she says.

On the screen a man has replaced the tragedy, the rescue. She has always found this man handsome: his pale eyebrows, vacant hair, endearing somehow. In color she imagines he might be florid, approaching the red of Sid, whom she now sees has found and uncorked the second bottle and is pouring himself a healthy glass.

"Et tu, Brute?" he says, the bottle poised, his shaky hand momentarily steady, accommodating. That Simone had found him so attractive Marie cannot quite understand, though she sees a certain something, or the remnants—the playboy, he had told them during Friendly Break, the raconteur, the Artist of the East Village, when that had meant more than now, before Starbucks, before the glassy tower condos, before everything changed.

"If I must," Marie says, watching Sid pour.*

––––––––––––

*The woods are cold and the sky is clear and from where she hides in the orchard, Marie has a view of a thousand stars. She will not sleep in the house; she cannot sleep in the house. The light had once been beautiful, the yellow of it lining the trees and the clouds where it caught the edge, the orange-apricot light so sharp she could barely open her eyes.

Tomorrow she will find her way elsewhere, but for right now, she is tired and sick and she sleeps in the retch of rotten fruit. Earlier she watched the neighbors come, St. Claire's wife from the rectory, her idiot sons, Dudam and Benoit; the neighbors Karwoski and Higgen and Fruchs, and the red-haired woman with her red-haired girls, dragging the cart the pony once pulled, the pony butchered for meat. Everyone knew the story. She watched as her neighbors stepped into her house and stepped out again, carrying the things that belonged to her family, the fiddle and the pot: her mother's loom. At first she kept track and then she did not. Then she closed her eyes and covered herself in the rank, loose leaves she found beneath the trees and slept, dreaming no dreams.

Who were they to be hunted? Marie had little idea. Perhaps her mother's eyes were too blue. Perhaps her father was a Communist. Her brother's spectacles: Was he blind? Crippled? Deaf? She remembers this: The kitchen still warm, fire embers in the stove. Her sisters' shoes lined against the wall near the umbrella stand, beneath the black-veined mirror framed in gold where she stood and saw the look on her own face: her pale cheeks, black eyebrows her sisters said would be modern if waxed thin, her forehead, too high, she once let on to her best friend. She looks at who she was but she can see nothing but the work boots, the umbrella stand, the mirror that once belonged to her grandparents in Paris, bought on a weekend trip to the Dordogne, to the cottage there beneath the castle. Her grandmother walked her to the view and told her about the days when knights had lived within the castle fortress and how the iron gates they passed through were to keep out the enemies. Her grandmother held her hand and gripped a walking stick for the climb, and when they reached the view it looked to her, she told her grandmother, as if someone had stitched together the land like a big quilt. Maybe God? she guessed, but her grandmother, leaning on her walking stick, did not say yes or no.

The mirror possibly was bought in one of the tiny towns in the Dordogne where her grandparents kept a cottage beneath a castle, the castle dark against the blue, blue sky, or the gray, gray sky. She walked in the village market with her grandmother; she held her grandmother's old hand and carried a string bag for the cabbages. Her grandfather was wild for cabbages, her grandmother told her, and Brussels sprouts and leeks. She planned a soup. She would need bread. She would need coffee. Do not let me forget the other things, her grandmother said. I always forget something.

Her mother's books. Latin. She taught the children in town and then she did not; then she stayed at home and made soup. Her father was wild for cabbages and Brussels sprouts and leeks.

Her job to slice the bread. She knew how to hold a knife. This way, her mother said. Her father came through the door to say the horses should be blanketed.

I can, she said, but he had already left.

Her sisters were soon to be brides. They wanted to marry the brothers they had already found, not the boys they might find somewhere else.

We are going, her father said.

Her mother's books: she taught Latin, history. She said, Prehistoric is before history. It is the age when little is known. She had been a schoolteacher and now she cooked. She was making stone soup in her magic soup pot, she said, wiping her eyes with her sleeve. Voilà, she said.

The Stone Age, she said, refers to the time when people learned how to use stones as tools, the time when they first figured things out, she said.

Her father came through the door to say the cold was bitter and already the dark. So early. A bird followed him in and flapped around the kitchen where her mother made the stone soup. Her father waited for the bird to land and then whispered something that sounded like shh, shh. The bird cocked its head as if listening. It perched on the shelf that held the flour and the sugar though there was no more flour and no more sugar. It cocked its head. Her father held out his hand, raw with cold, flat, toward the bird perched on the empty shelf and everything was still and warm and she knew she loved her father and her mother best and they loved her. She watched her parents waiting for the bird and when the bird hopped onto her father's palm she closed her eyes and wished for everything.

The bird sailed out the door. The bird sailed out the window. They ate the bird for dinner.

She helped her mother with the stone soup. She gathered all the stones she could find. She was not under any circumstances to cross into the rectory orchard. She was not under any circumstances to speak to Dudam or Benoit, to leave the shadows of their own house. She was to do her job and return quick as a rabbit. Did she understand?

She found the stones beneath the moss, embedded in the moss: tiny perfect orange and white and pink pebbles, perfectly delicious. She picked the pebbles from the moss like crumbs from a plate. She smelled the rotting fruit from the rectory orchard and her mouth watered. She licked her fingers and picked the pebbles until she had a skirtful. The pebbles were from the Stone Age, her mother told her. From the glaciers that defined the mountains, lakes, and valleys of the earth. Did she remember the Stone Age? her mother said. We are living in the Stone Age, her mother said. We must figure things out.

Her sisters cried because the boys they were to marry had run away. The boys had put on disguises and sewn treasures into the bottoms of their hard-soled shoes. Beyond looked better now to the sisters but now was too late.

Besides, they did not own hard-soled shoes, only work boots split at the toe and heel.

Be quiet, their mother said, or I will make shoe soup.

Their mother wiped her eyes with her sleeve.

I like stone soup best, one of her sisters said.

Better than chicken with dumplings, her other sister said.

Better than leeks and Brussels sprouts, her mother said.

They all three laughed and she did not understand what was so funny: she sat with a lap full of pebbles picking out the bad ones as if she were cleaning beans.

Her brother, Ernest, read in the corner. She liked a quiet place to read. She liked school. They had closed the school and sent her mother home with all her Latin books and history books.

The Egyptians were the ones, her mother said. They really figured things out.

Her mother piled up the good pebbles into a pyramid and then she poked a hole in the pyramid and the pebbles fell again, scattering.

The neighbors took her mother's soup pot. They took the ancient mirror and the umbrella stand. They took her father's tools and led his two horses from the barn steaming cold. She watched them from her hiding place in the rectory orchard. The neighbors did not see her though they slunk about as if watched by something: they shuttled in and out like water rats, she thought. If that one dropped the magic soup pot she could make rat soup.

Rat soup would be delicious, she thought.

She would figure things out.

When the blue-dark went black she snuck back in to find what they had left but they had left nothing and so she went to the woods where her father had once told her she would find good fairies if she needed protection.

He said the word *protection* and she had no idea.

"Knock, knock," Sid Morris says. "Are you sleeping?"

Marie opens her eyes. The pain branches out and flowers in places where there should be no pain, up her spine, across her shoulders. The doctor called it reflective pain, as if pain were a thing with a face. "It hurts," she says.

---

The woods were dark and cold like the fairy tales her father sometimes read to her at night. She liked history better. The Ice Age. She had a book called *The Dawn of Mankind* with illustrations drawn in pen and ink—ice forming, ice melting, giant creatures receding and emerging. Not so far from here, her mother said, our ancestors painted pictures of animals that no longer even exist. They did not paint them to remember them but to imagine them into being. If they painted them, they believed, the animals would show up and then they could kill and eat them.

In the dark woods she sat against the spruce where before she had watched the orange-apricot light so sharp she had to close her eyes. The dark there behind her eyes was as dark as a cave and as cold because her mother had said to see the pictures painted in the cave you must wear your mittens and your coats, all of them, and wrap your neck in scarves. It is very cold in the caves where our ancestors painted their pictures and they must have been shivering when they imagined the animals that would save them. She shivered and imagined, painting pictures of the good fairies with her hand that did not hold the bad pebbles. The fairies had shiny wings and golden hair; they wore flower-blossom clothing—trumpet vine caps and skirts of white rose petals and pink morning glories. They smelled sweet. On the wet, cold cave wall the fairies glowed and from time to time one of them flapped off the cave wall and darted around the dark cave until she held out her hand, quietly, and the fairy hopped on, and she said, shh, shh.

She opened her eyes to see a man with a thick beard and hat who said, shh, shh, and with him a woman who held out a horse blanket. She could smell the horse but she could not see in the dark. She did not know whether she was in the woods or in her mind's eyes imagining but still she went because she was cold and it was dark and she felt very much alone.

# XV

Sid Morris stands to clear and wash the dishes, the soapy water turned blue from the paint still on his hands. He should leave after this; he should find his way home. He had been coming to express his condolences, Simone's death having reached the School of Inspired Arts late by way of Duane Reade, who had heard because pharmacists hear things, he said, his pale eyebrows nearly disappeared, the mustache, thicker, dyed and waxed; it stood out against his face, which stood out against his lab coat.

Duane Reade leaned in. The stories I could tell, he said. Addictions, he said. Murder. Creepy stuff, he said, leaning back and staring Sid Morris full in the face.

Another time, Sid Morris said. Cold and they were on the busy corner of Twenty-Fifth and Eighth.

Sid Morris had assumed Simone temporarily felled by a setback of one sort or another, not death. They came and went, these old women; their bones brittle, requiring stitching, physical therapy; they had surgeries to excise tumors, suspicious lesions; or they left for months to care for grandchildren, putting their own lives on hold, stepping aside so the real passengers could take their seats.

He has seen it all with Veritas. Poof! Or, how had she put it? A momentary sabbatical. A year, maybe two. She needed to think. She needed to reaccess, using one of those store-bought terms you never heard below Fourteenth Street, not where he grew up, not from the mouths of his parents. His mother's hands, he could tell you. What she hadn't seen. And the hospice worker calling to express her condolences at his mother's death leaving a message on a machine saying she would be happy to talk if he needed any comfort as he moved through the grief process. Grief process. Shit.

His first thought on hearing from Duane Reade of Simone's passing: her lovely skin, so soft—a secret, she had said; and her general smells, her powders—all gone.*

He had kissed her wrists.

"Do I repulse you?" he asked. She shivered.

"Why on earth would you say that?"

"I am a man," he said, inexplicably.

"Me, too," she said. "I mean, a woman," she said.

He had kissed the tributary of veins on her wrist. Where had they been? Madison Square Park, a walk. A thawing winter day, some snowdrops already in the warm spots. Flowers in Decem-

---

*The powders were caked in tubes or pressed into compacts from the fifties, their plastic clamshell lids and palm-size mirrors flecked with black. How many times had her mother seen her own face in these, and now only Katherine looking back, a stouter version of her mother, more her father's build, stocky, short-waisted, but in this mirror none of that, only her face, pretty like her mother's though not as pretty, not nearly as pretty, she thinks, dumping the tubes and the compacts, the dried-out mascaras and spent lipsticks, the beveled-glass bottles of perfume—some nearly empty, others almost full— and the one her father gave her mother every year for Christmas, her mother pretending she had no idea, squealing like a little girl—into a cardboard box she believed she would throw out but on which she later wrote with Sharpie, MOTHER.

her! So odd! she had said. She loved the yellow crocus best; he, purple. Flowers!

Sid Morris had asked the Thursday class to stand for a minute of silence. The model donned her Chinese robe. The students shuffled up, Helen quietly tearful; she had grown fond of the two old Frenchwomen, the way they hurried in, late, the walk, they apologized, longer than they anticipated given the bad weather and, Simone would say, their waning sense of direction—she the talker of the two, so that Helen now understands she will not see Marie again, either; Marie too shy, or maybe something else: pensive, or maybe just not as interested, although it was to Marie that Helen had felt the stronger kinship, Marie's imagination—the forests and odd animals, the sense Marie had been trying to paint something lost to the world, or not yet imagined; something difficult to picture, almost impossible.

The group waited, awkward, Duane Reade the most bent out of shape—he had assumed he would bear the news. But Sid Morris did not notice. He suggested they face east toward the Woolworth Building, the Empire State, the East River, and the contested Brooklyn Waterfront Greenway, and then he watched the clock, a full minute—endless—before he began.

"We are here to remember our good friend and fellow artist, Simone," he said. But that was wrong; none of them were here for that; they were here to paint, to replicate the model's stance, to see in the way one must see to be alive. We are here, then, to be alive. To live. Ironic, Sid Morris thought, given the circumstances. This all in the span of gathering his thoughts, of attempting to picture Simone's face in his mind's eye though he pictured only a fur coat too heavy for a woman as old as she, too heavy for him to hold at that dinner a hundred years ago, or maybe last week—time folding in on itself at his age, weightless, fleeting.

"Devoted wife," Sid Morris continued. "Kind mother," he said, rushing it closed as Veritas rose up to accuse him of everything.

"Amen," he said. "Amen," the gathered said, the model's amen especially loud, almost strident as she dropped her robe and resumed her position on the claw-footed divan, a droopy slouch, one leg crossed over the other, head back as if in ecstasy. As if in ecstasy, Sid Morris had earlier instructed. You know ecstasy, right, dear? he said as the model looked back bored at the dirty old man.

# XVI

But it appears Sid Morris has no intention of leaving. They sit in the dark backyard in twin wrought iron chairs, white-painted, rusting, their springs long sprung. Hold still, he says, balancing his cigarette in the old clamshell on the matching table and propping Marie's cast in his lap. It had been Sid's idea to paint her cast, to make her an original Sid Morris. She listens to him now and tries not to breathe as directed. She has taken more for the pain and the wine, too, so the pain is a muffled bell she detects in the distance: someone late for dinner. Sid Morris picks up the cigarette again, inhaling then flicking ash, the smoke dribbling from his nose, its familiar smell sharp, nostalgic in a way that surprises her.

Next door the movie star's floodlight, fixed over the movie star's back door, lights his forsythia and birch like museum pieces, his backyard awash in contrast, treasure and not, pools of ink its corners and on its roof, unseen, the movie star declaiming—this his late-night habit, Marie has explained to Sid Morris. You get used to it, she says. (The need for space alone: the babies, the new house, new wife.)

"Alas, sir," they hear, and then, "Horatio," or something. Is it

Horatio? Could it possibly be, Horatio? Or maybe, Mercutio? He has moved through several tragedies and now, apparently, is to finally appear onstage. He hopes she will see him.

They stand near her front stoop. That close she feels how the movie star is buoyed by extra air. She has just returned from the fruit vendor, a plastic bag of plums looped to her wrist. People who pass turn to be sure he is who he is though they do not quite believe their eyes so they turn again, and then again.

"And those?" Sid Morris is asking.

"Privets. Abe liked topiary. He used to sculpt them: that one's a chick."

She had led Sid Morris to the back door—his suggestion, the backyard, he needed a smoke, fresh air—and pushed up the policeman's bolt to the balmy night, the wet rush of traffic, the possible crickets already—too early—and Roscoe from nowhere, the beggar, in a rush back in. "Shoo," Marie said. "Shoo," she said.

They sat in the rusted wrought-iron chairs, his cigarette the only color in the dark: orange where he settled in, something to follow, his breath. She sat across from him. The grass wet, the seat cushions wet: dew, or mist, and on the table the old clamshell for ash puddled; he knocked the water out. Yesterday rain, tomorrow even more and a new storm brewing. Just last week some bulbs rose from the dirt with weak white shoots, molding, soft to touch, or maybe the dirt just washed away. And who are you? she had said to them. My tulips? My narcissus?

At a great distance, the steady toll of the bell, the pain. She turns her cast in Sid Morris's lap so he can better see. Earlier, in the muted light of one of the fringed lamps from a certain dynasty—sixty-watt, Abe had insisted, so as not to scorch the silk—Sid Morris chose colors and a brush from her tackle box, Very Grand rising as if she might swoop down and take a bite.

"Do you miss him?" Sid is saying; his hair, too long at the collar, and the way his braces crisscross his shoulders.

"Every minute," she says.

He concentrates, biting his lip. He wears the same dirty shirt he wore when they first met. Months ago now; one lifetime: Simone standing with Henry's Brooklyn Bridge, already flirting.*

---

*The man with the thick beard and the woman unwrapped her in a warm place. In the dark she felt her own shivering. The woman rubbed her legs with warm hands. Someone lit a candle. She was in a shop of some sort, photographs on the walls, portraits of people sitting for portraits, men and women and little children arranged like fruit on a raked wooden table, children looking serious and strange, dressed in their best dress. They did not look like her parents or like Ernest and Rose and Sylvie. She thought of Ernest and Rose and Sylvie and then she did not; she shut her eyes hard and the woman spoke to her and said she would bring her a cup of tea now that she looked awake and maybe it would not be too hot to taste and would that be fine?

Marie nodded, a mouse nod.

She might be a little mouse in someone's pocket; she might burrow into a fluff of cotton. She would like to speak but she is a mouse and so can only squeak.

Don't, the woman said to her little mouse voice. Don't speak.

The woman came back and put a cup of tea into her tiny mouse hands, her tiny claws, and the woman held the tea as well so that Marie would not spill it because she was shaking, shivering, and the tea felt too hot and so she coughed.

I'm sorry, she said in her real voice.

And the woman said to the man, Too soon.

And then the woman said something else to the man that Marie did not understand, something in a language she did not understand, and then the man picked her up again and carried her through a smaller door to a dark room where there were no portraits only boxes stacked upon boxes and a wooden table and chair and a cot and here the man set her down and the woman came behind with blankets and said, Sleep.

And Marie nodded.

And the woman asked her name but Marie had turned into a tiny mouse, again, like the kind that used to sneak into the kitchen when her mother made stone soup. Nothing for you, little mouse, her mother would say. Not even a crumb. And Marie would watch the mouse circle around and around, looking for anything, and then scurry away, back into the hole beneath the floorboards where sometimes, if her father had earned some of the hard cracker bread or a neighbor took pity, she would slip a crumb down so that the mouse might have more than stone soup for its dinner, too. When Marie waked she thought for a moment she might be back in her old house, or maybe in the dark of the orchard; it was very dark here. She felt sore beneath the soft blankets, and hungry, and then her eyes cleared and she saw the woman sitting next to her, in the wooden chair, at the wooden table, looking at her as sometimes her own mother looked at her while she slept.

Good morning, the woman said.

Good morning, Marie said, surprised by her own voice.

You speak, the woman said.

Yes, she said.

I am Colette.

Marie.

Marie, Colette said.

Somewhere beyond them the sound of water, a faucet turned on and then off. Maybe shuffling.

It is Sunday today and we'll have no customers, Colette said.

She did not understand Colette, and she did not understand where she was but it was warm beneath the blanket. Her eyes saw through the dark like a cat, saw the grain sacks like the ones her father had for the horses over the windows and the wooden table and the wooden chairs and saw, in the corner, the tripod though she did not know the name. She remembered how once she went with Mother and Ernest to the place where Rose and Sylvie sat for the man who took their pictures. This must be that kind of place.

This is his studio. We don't live here, Colette says. People come and sit. Even now. Last week Coco Pellet. You know her? A great favorite. Carné's muse, they say. Last week she waltzed in soldier on her arm. An officer. Maybe she on his arm, like a Cartier. He had these eyes. He said he wanted Coco Pellet's portrait. Nude, he said. You imagine? Jules said, this is not a penny arcade. Sometimes he forgets. He forgets and works, forgetting. Coco Pellet said nothing. You could see her collarbones. She gave her cigarette to the officer and said let's go and they walked out, thank God. Usually he knows what to say. He is smart. This time he was a fool.

Colette pauses a moment, looking out toward the window as if admiring a view though the only thing to see is the sack, burlap, tacked across it, the way the burlap filters the day.

This is our darkroom. We can stop them from looking here. Jules is well known and they are vain men. They want a portrait. Something to send back home: their girlfriends, their mothers. They are little boys. They want to remember the beautiful women. Idiots.

In the near dark Colette walks to the door and when she opens it stark light comes from the other room, the shop where it may be daylight, suppertime. Marie waits, shivering. She might get up from here quickly and climb out one of the windows or she might hide under the bed but the woman Colette seemed more like her mother than anyone she should be afraid of. Do not be afraid of everyone, her mother had said to her. Do not make her afraid of everyone, her mother had said to her father. What kind of life is this? her mother had said to her father.

In the famous cave of Lascaux, her mother said, a little train takes you into the dark and you cannot see and then you can—they have candles—and it is very cold and the colors are like no colors because they have never been seen and the animals are four-headed or flying with wings, dragons, and they are all creatures drawn by persons from the imagination. All the things we cannot know and wish for maybe.

Her mother's eyes are blue. Her father sometimes smokes a pipe.

Now, Colette says. She has walked back through the door of light and is here, again.

We'll go slowly, she says. She puts the bowl on the table next to the bed and then she pulls Marie up. Marie can sit. Colette props the pillow behind her back and then she holds the bowl in her own hand and gives Marie a spoon or takes the spoon and scoops and helps Marie to carry the spoon to her mouth.

Slowly, Colette says.

It is difficult to swallow and she spits, and then she does swallow, the soup pressed down her throat as if by hands, one and then two, squeezing, squeezing, the soup must go down, the stones, one and then two and then three, they are magic stones and they will weigh her to the ground so that when the others fly away she will still be here.

She is still here.

I am still here, she says.

Yes, Colette says.

Colette wipes her mouth with the apron she wears. She scoops the soup into her mouth; she is not a mouse but a bird, a tiny baby bird.

At night we go to the woods. That is where we found you. We go to the woods and meet people there. We do not know their names, we cannot know their names; we give them papers. It is all arranged. We give them the papers Jules makes. The watermark. The stamp. All kinds of papers—birth and baptism. ID cards. He has a special dust. I don't know how he does it. Jules says I should stay behind but I do not want to be left and so I go. He cannot make me stay home. We have no children. I cannot or he cannot but we have none and so I would be alone and I would rather die.

Maybe your father once met him. Maybe your mother, who knows?

Colette wipes her mouth, again. She will soon draw a bath, she tells her. She is filthy though too young to smell, maybe eight? Nine? She has a rash on her legs. Her eyes are blue, which is good. Jules will photograph her later, after she has had more sleep, a bit more to eat, she says. You will clean up nicely, she says, and we will put you in the dress that will fit, the white one with the pearly buttons down the back and the sky-blue ribbon and the hat to match, an Easter outfit, a bonnet, and Jules can take your photograph like the ones in the lockets, the miniatures that were so popular when I was a little girl your age, miniatures we put into tiny gold hearts that would pop open with tiny clasps. You will like Madame Brouchard. Your likeness to her girls extraordinary. Jules has even said it and he doesn't say much. They are good people.

"What?" Marie says. The medication has made her very tired, a bit out of it: the day, the evening. She no longer sleeps but if she did this is how it would feel: exhaustion. Sid Morris is talking.

"I was saying when I was a kid we had a teacher. Shivers," Sid Morris says. "That's what we called him, as in shiver me timbers. Anything, he'd jump out of his skin. France, though I didn't know squat."

"France," she says.

"We were shits. We'd slam our books. Push them off our desks. Then we'd say, Sorry, Mr. Shivers."

"Terrible," Marie says.

"I was the worst," Sid Morris says, stubbing out the last of the cigarette, the old clamshell saved from a party in Red Hook—forgotten friends who lived close to the docks, she remembers

"One day our principal's at Shivers's desk. Open your books, he says, some chemistry bullshit. And that was that. No Shivers. And no one had the balls to ask."

"What happened?" Marie asks.

Sid Morris shrugs. "Who knows?"

Sid Morris wets the tip of the brush in his mouth.

"I never thought about Shivers," he says. "All these years and now I'm thinking about Shivers. All the time I'm thinking about Shivers. Even now, here," Sid Morris says, painting something she cannot see. "I'm thinking about Shivers."

In the dark, dark, beyond the movie star's floodlight, the newly bloomed forsythia hides a swarm of ghost spiders spinning webs, their spinning systems on overdrive, ramped by the frenzy of the City's vibrations: subway crossings, thermal energy, steam, plumbing, satellites, fleets of taxis, and down the street, on the farthest corner at the Rawhide, the regular men of ladies' night dance and dance, refusing to believe the bar's impending closing: they dance in two-for-one oblivion, dance like all get-out in their get-ups, pedestrians crisscrossing the thronged bicycle lanes, impossible passages, the delivery boys and muscle boys and pretty women who work at magazines weaving in and out of the stalled traffic on Citi Bikes, on foot, this a balmy almost-spring spring night, or close to it, an intimation of what will come—heat, almost tropical, rain falling in sheets, trash bins brimming, washed away, eddying—too much stuff; too many people to count.

"Fuck, Shivers," Sid Morris suddenly says. "What kind of *meshuga* backyard with so little light?" He strikes a match for another cigarette. She can feel the heat of his lap through her cast or maybe she is just imagining. Far away, in history, the bell rings, the child hiding up a tree. But she will not go home and she will not go home and even though the bell clangs she will never go home.

"Hello? Hello?" Sid Morris says, knocking on her cast with his free hand. "Are you with me?"

"I'm here," she says. "I'm still here," she says.

# XVII

After Elizabeth won the small prize in graduate school, the entire department gathered, students and faculty, in the lounge to hear her read, the refreshments generously donated by the surplus at History, a department better-funded for reasons having to do with the tragedy of Miles Whitbread.

Elizabeth looked out from the little half-podium hastily set up on the conference table, and then she did what they had gathered to see her do, although moments before she had believed she just might faint. Still, she read, shakily, the four poems she had labored over for her three years of graduate school.

Three years, she thought, even while reading. Four poems, she thought. That was all she wrote.

"The end," she said, looking up, smiling.

The applause surprised her, delighted her. She might have even said sustained. Hernandez approached first, beaming. "Brava," he said. "Brava!"

She gave a little bow and a curtsy; she wore a skirt of her own making. Long ago she'd gotten used to stitching together

fabric into skirts, sundresses, smocks when outings with her
mother meant Woolworth's for a grilled cheese and coffee and
the bible of patterns in back, the fabric swatches on sale.*

"I need a drink!" Elizabeth said.

"Here, here," someone said to her left and then she had a
Dixie cup of white wine. "Cheese?" they said, and she saw Rich-
ard, the Brit, a speared orange cube on a pick. She should have
known; should have heard the voice.

---

*She loved best the black-lined jaunty women, angular and sharp, their
clothes set off with a neat hat or fluffy poodle on a leash. Illustrations of how
it should all turn out if you followed the directions. She would follow the directions. She would cut along the dotted lines then deftly stitch so she could
match them, these women in their smart suits and A-line jackets, their belted
trench coats and high, slender boots. She had learned how to follow directions in Home Ec and knew exactly what to do. She unfolded the papery patterns inside the packages and cut along the dotted lines with sharp scissors;
pinning the pins, the tiny colored balls straight or almost so the machine's
threading would not crush them. She had written a poem about it called "How
It Should All Turn Out": it was the best of the four poems. She had written it
quickly, sitting on her bed in the top-floor studio of the three-story Victorian on
Elm she rented for $450 a month. Roaches in the sink and a cat who perched
atop the kitchen cabinets, peering down as she composed at her small, round
table, Pete elsewhere for the time being, the two taking a break for graduate
school, they'd agreed. She had a plan. She would get her master's. She would
marry Pete. She would work in marketing or public relations, writing poetry on
the side: income as well as tiny, perfect bonsais, compositions of what it all
meant. Maybe even a collection or three. What she did not say was *penance,*
though this is what her mother heard. They walked in silence. Her mother
would later say she loved the gray stone and stained glass of all the empty
churches near the Elm Street studio. Elizabeth would later say she liked the
linden trees but little else, the entire town gloomy and worn down, as if all the
weight of all its books were balanced on its scholarly shoulders, weak from
lack of exercise.

"No, this is perfect. Cheers," she said, downing her thimble and immediately reaching for more. "I'm parched," she said.

"You're amazing," he said, pouring.

"Go on," she said, looking around for Hernandez but he had wandered off, again.

"You are," he said. "The real deal." The Brit's eyes were green and freckled like the Irish—was he Irish? He had a smooth voice, a beautiful voice. His poems she never fully understood but others did and pronounced them brilliant; he would have won the small prize, she knew, would have beat her had he been in her own class, but he had only just arrived.

"You, too," she said, gregarious. She felt a sudden whoosh of affection for everyone who had listened to her three years, four poems, anyone who stood now with wilted napkins and cheese and warm wine in the center of this room, littered with journals and reviews.

Years later, she will recognize the Brit's name on a panel of distinguished Brits and think maybe she should show up and ask a question from the back. Or maybe she should just sit there and smile.

Who would come to hear him?

Who really has the time?

He sees a stranger among familiar faces and is puzzled—he knows he knows her from somewhere—but it isn't until afterward, when she approaches him, that he puts two and two together, launching forth on their graduate school, the ones he's seen the ones he's read about the ones he's lost track of given his distance across the pond.

And what of you? he would like to know. Tell! he says.

But this isn't about that, Elizabeth thinks, standing in the administrative hallway, the checkerboard Who We Ares lining the painted cement walls. This is about how it all turned out for

the rest of them. What do the rest of them say? What do they
think? Carol Weisman, for instance. How did it all turn out for
Carol Weisman?

Elizabeth leans in to examine the photograph of Carol Weisman linked to her husband, the myopic Ethan, and their twin
boys. They stand on a beach somewhere in the Caribbean, the
boys and Ethan holding spears. Ethan took up spearfishing on
this vacation, teaching his sons, notorious troublemakers at Progressive K–8, how to spike flounder with one jab. But what did
Carol do while her boys were out fishing? Did she paint her toenails? Read Thomas Hardy in the bath? Jog? It seems important,
somehow, the most important detail: What Occupied Carol's
Time While the Boys Went Fishing.*

Elizabeth reads it all again in the pinprick of light cast by
her slender flashlight, something Pete keeps in the top kitchen
drawer in a box marked CONTINGENCIES. This is certainly a con-
tingency, Elizabeth thinks, although what has led her here, what
she intends to do, is as much a mystery to her as Ethan's pinched
smile, Carol's sunburned squint. There's something to be discovered; something more to be said. She reads as if looking for
the clues to what, the bread crumbs that might lead her there.

---

*They couldn't have been more different: Ethan's only-child childhood in
Manhattan, the East Seventies, his three years prepping at St. Paul's, his
time at Yale before Harvard Law, his summers in Europe, while Carol, the
fourth of five daughters of a sunflower grower in southern Indiana (the Sunflower King!), majored in communications at the University of Illinois before
escaping to New York. Her ancestors were of German descent, Carol wrote,
men and women who left their country in the early nineteenth century and
found themselves in Ohio and then Indiana, a fertile land they immediately
recognized as perfect for sunflowers—Ethan's relatives, on the other hand,
were Ashkenazi Jews. But on their blind date they had talked for hours, and
only months later decided to tie the knot.

Or here, to the left, where Matty and Vicky Tange have been professionally arranged on the steps of an old-timey veranda within pots of erupting geraniums: Vicky in a sleeveless dress and pearls, stick-thin, her wife, Matty, at her side, their daughter, Kristi, adopted from China at fourteen months, dressed as if for a tea party, frilly skirt, frilly top, white gloves, in Matty's arms.

She came to us as if in a dream, Matty's written. We dreamt her first. I woke Vicky and said, Kristi.

Vicky said, What?

Let's call her Kristi, I said.

Let's call who Kristi? Vicky said. Vicky's always the last to know!

It took us months to complete the paperwork and then we were literally on a slow boat to China. Or plane! Kristi met us at the gates of the orphanage. Orphanage D-13. There were chickens and I remember the sound of roosters. When you adopt a child, you do not look at her and think, Is this my child? You look at her and think, Oh, here you are.

Here you are, Elizabeth reads, and once again feels the catch in her throat.

# XVIII

Sometimes, in the early evenings and into their cups, Mr. and Mrs. Whitbread speculate what their Miles might have become had he not foolishly chosen to get behind the wheel of that automobile when he did, though *foolishly* is not a word that Mr. and Mrs. Whitbread would use: Had he been foolish? No. Just tired and overworked, understanding too well what would be required from his studies in the weeks and months ahead and wanting no part of it though of course wanting everything, the world and all its possibilities round and sweet as one of those jawbreakers he loved as a kid; he could almost taste its sweet as he sucked it down to nothing. He was a boy to whom everything came easily and yet also a boy who understood this about himself and knew, in his fingertips, how fortunate he seemed to anyone looking in—this mattered to Miles. It mattered a lot. As a student of history, his *passion*, he said to the friends of Mr. and Mrs. Whitbread's who sought out Miles at the Whitbreads' well-attended New Year's Day open house (the daughters, Lucy and Janet, shy and for the most part assisting the hired help pass), guests who wanted to hear what Miles, now a senior at college and remembered as the valedictorian of the high school class, the captain of the crew team, the sometimes date for their daughters, had up his sleeve.

"History," Miles said. "I want to understand the place of history in our lives," Miles said, always earnest, repeating the name of the senior seminar in which he averaged an A. *Understanding the Place of History in Our Lives*, the course book read, its instructor a former member of the foreign service turned mystery writer, a Skull and Bones type who frankly got a kick out of working with the students and would have done it for free, or paid *them*, he said. Miles Whitbread quoted his professor freely at the Whitbreads' New Year's Day gathering. Had one or two of the guests expressed any interest in history, Miles Whitbread might have even read to them the opening paragraphs of his final paper for the class, a paper on the topic of his great-uncle already in its third or fourth draft.*

---

*In 1953, on a frozen hill somewhere above the Thirty-Eighth Parallel in what was then Korea, my great-uncle Atticus Charles Whitbread, known as Whit Charles, stood among the cobbled UN forces, the best among them a group of Ethiopians. The men watched as the colonel, nicknamed Shorty, led a cow toward his bunker, warmer than the trenches Whit Charles and the others dug and lived in, shooting rats from the tips of their boots on moonlit nights and on moonless nights picturing worse. Earlier that day, the Chinese had taken Hill 454, or Marilyn Monroe, as they called it. Whit Charles had watched to the north as a soldier shit in a can; he didn't want to look to the east, where the crucified boy's face, Air Force, had swollen to the size of a pumpkin. Now the sun had set and left the bitter cold. There was a dusting of snow. The men shivered in their trenches, the Ethiopians speaking a language Whit Charles could not understand. They had beautiful hands and moved them as they spoke as if carving air. Their eyes were wide and white. They were thin as switches and Whit Charles watched as their leader bent down and used his knife to scrape something off his boot before licking the blade with his long red tongue. The next day the Ethiopians were dead but my great-uncle was still alive. Random is the place of history in our lives.

Mr. and Mrs. Whitbread found a copy of the draft of their son's paper tucked in his hunting jacket pocket. The police had given the jacket to the Whitbreads along with the keys and the mints and the school ID and the packet of condoms and peeled skin of an orange found in the glove compartment, the hunting jacket folded in the backseat, they explained, untouched. Indeed the backseat of the automobile looked like the backseat of an automobile anywhere, books and papers, a hockey stick. The automobile sheared in half, scissored just like that, so that if you were to open the back door you might think you were fine. The drunk had opened the back door, stumbling out of his own automobile without a scratch. He had opened the back door thinking it the front door, relieved to see no one there and therefore, he had wrongly assumed, no one dead or dying.

The drunk had crawled into the backseat of the automobile and fallen asleep. When the police arrived on the scene they were baffled by the man asleep in the backseat, thinking him Miles's passenger though Miles was very much alone, dead in the front seat, shorn and crushed against a sugar maple several hundred yards away.*

---

*In addition to the death of Miles Whitbread, this same sugar maple had been responsible for the births of hundreds of robins and the deflowering of a virgin named Sophie, who, when she saw how her boyfriend Tray had carved I LOVE SOPHIE in the bark of its trunk in the autumn of 1973, had been so moved as to forget her vow of chastity until marriage, something she had discussed at length with her girlfriends and only later confessed to betraying—the sex sweet: after a picnic and before a rainstorm, the air taut with atmosphere, some kind of rejiggering so that, in later years, Sophie associated weather with desire: a little randy she'd say to her boyfriends, her husband, her lovers, given any tiny shift in barometric pressure, until she grew so old and dry that neither hurricane nor northeaster could interest her at all.

What if he were with a friend, if he hadn't been driving? Mrs. Whitbread would say—this after midnight, into her cups, the Whitbreads, social people, had been out somewhere, had returned to their sunroom, ringed, as they were, by framed photographs of Miles and Lucy and Janet.

"What if he had stayed home? Then he would not have been in the car at all," Mr. Whitbread would say.

The Whitbreads sit in their sunroom, the only room easily heated, electric.

"Or what if he had asked his friend to drive?" Mrs. Whitbread would say.

"Right," Mr. Whitbread would say.

"I wish he had," Mrs. Whitbread would say.

"Yes," Mr. Whitbread would say.

# XIX

Jules and Larry stand at the door. "It's freezing!" Jules says. "When did New York get so cold?"

"You're here!" Marie says.

"I told you I would so I did. We did. Besides, you never answer your phone. Anyway, it's April, isn't it? Christ it's cold."

"Come in, come in," she says. "Oh my," she says. "What a surprise." Larry squeezes past perfumed, a wool scarf of bold university colors wrapped around his neck. "I need a heater," he says.

"Quick," she says. "I'll make tea."

Jules is next, looking more and more the spitting image; she finds it difficult not to say, Abe. He has not stood in this hallway for some time and now he's here: Abe, Jules. Jules stands tall, like his father, his hair Abe's once blond, curly, already gray.

"Your hands are frigid!" Marie says.

"We got the first flight we could manage. I can't believe you didn't tell me."

"This place is amazing," Larry says, returning. "I love the blue." He has his coat off, and Marie sees he wears a white shirt and tie.

"Larry likes to dress to travel," Jules says. "It's a dying art."

"You look wonderful," Marie says. "You both look wonderful and look at me," she says. She stands in housecoat and slippers—it is too early. She had no idea. They must have flown overnight. They must be exhausted. She makes them follow her to the kitchen, Jules insisting on giving Larry a tour now, where he slept as a boy, where he slept as a teenager, though that part, the top floor, is occupied by the tenants. "You'll hear them tomorrow morning," Jules tells Larry. "Very loud. There's always a commotion. Don't they have, like, five little kids?"

"One," Marie says. "And he's already a teenager."

"I remember it as five," Jules says. "And possibly dogs."

Marie says she'll boil the eggs and please stop: she is not an invalid. She's perfectly all right. A tiny fracture: on the screen a scratch you wouldn't notice. She's old. Bones break. It's all a bore. She'd been surprised by the cast. It's all so dumb and stupid. She'll have none of it, this show. She's just happy for their company and how long will they stay?

"Unclear," Jules says. He's all legs and arms. "Larry's got something but we'll see," he says.*

"Mom?" Jules says. But here the water's boiled away to nearly nothing.

"Let me do it," Jules says.

"A nine-minute egg," Larry says, laughing. "Perfect."

Outside Roscoe balances on the high dividing fence, his tail quivering. In the garden some forsythia spray yellow, and there are already daffodils. Next door the movie star's birch will

---

*He had Abe's curly hair, his broad shoulders. He loved men, not women. They knew before he told them; Abe wept, his shoulders shaking. He loved his Jules. He scooped him up in his strong arms and kissed Jules's toes until Jules dissolved from it: Jules loved his father best.

be the first to green, and then the few pears that still line the
street despite the storms and the moving vans that break their
branches, the pears planted, Marie remembers, by the block
association—the ones who put on the caroling—formed when
the neighborhood was dangerous, when somebody's wife was
mugged: bulbs in the fall, impatiens in spring, the children with
trowels digging the sparse dirt at the roots, careful not to nick.
"I am impatient with impatiens," Abe announced though he and
Jules were happy those Saturdays, dirt on their knees, beneath
their fingernails, in the creases of their palms so that Jules pre-
dicted he could read Abe's whole life there.


"Please let's not get into this now," Marie says.

"There are a million reasons but let me name three: Zone A,
Zone A, Zone A. I couldn't live with myself if you floated out
to the Hudson."

"There are worse ways to go," Marie says. The boys—she
can't help but call them this—have had a nap, a shower. The
sun is high, but weak. They sit in back somewhat revived, full of
pep, Larry says, petting Roscoe, who has jumped down to their
side.

"So, this is really his cat?" Larry says, changing the subject.

"One and the same," Marie says. "You'll see him around. He
sometimes rehearses on his roof."

"I fucking love New York," Larry says. "Sorry," he says.

"And what if you were injured in any way, or lost power for
a week? They don't know what will happen next. Get out. Dad
would have said so."

"It's weather," Marie says. "I survived the Blitz."

"Mother was there, I told you," Jules says to Larry. "Then she
found her way here."

"I thought you said Rochester," Larry says, admiring Roscoe. In a different life, the cat might have been a raccoon—blacks and browns and white, his tail ringed.

"London then Rochester then Dad then New York," Jules says.

"I got the sequence wrong," Larry says, pulling Roscoe to his lap. "Sue me."

"I wasn't criticizing."

"That's a first."

It had been Larry's idea to take the red-eye, to reach Jules's mother as soon as they could—she's hobbling around Chelsea at eighty-seven, he had said.

Eighty-five, Jules had said.

Whatever. The point is she's a target for a lunatic.

Lunatics can no longer afford Chelsea, Jules said.

"You're wrong about your father," Marie says.

"What? I thought you met him in Rochester?"

"About him wanting me to leave," Marie says. "This was our home."

Roscoe leaps from Larry's lap to the still-hard ground, the crimped green bulb shoots like so many broken fingers, matted clumps still matted by the dead leaves of winter. This year she hasn't yet raked, another reason Jules will say: the upkeep.*

---

*A thousand pigeons rise in Roscoe's wake and above, in the windows of the Stalin-era leviathan, apartments 15A and B, the idiot sons of St. Claire, Dudam and Benoit, pull aside the draperies, their greasy bangs and noses to the window watching as the soldiers force the neighbors out. Distracted by their foggy breath, the boys draw angels on the rippled glass, their nails sharp as quills.

# XX

"I don't know why," Elizabeth tells the policeman, Carlos, who apprehends her as she climbs the stairs to the Progressive K–8 art room—her intent finding spray paint, or maybe only a brush and oils. "I guess I was going to write something."

Stop, he had yelled, as if she were a criminal, and she had turned to see a policeman standing at the base of the stairs, his hand poised, or maybe just too close, to his gun.

Given the heightened alert of the City, the looming storms, the melting subterranean freeze, and the speed at which the oceans are rising, their currents no longer predictable, the police have come to suspect that anything can and most likely will happen. Every day they drill their What Ifs:

What If a Pandemic?
What If Manhattan were put under quarantine?
What If terrorists arrived by submarine?
What If the power grid goes?
What If a Biological Event were introduced?

The point is, someone has seen something and said something: something at Progressive K–8, a darting light in the shuttered windows. The police have been notified. Carlos eventually arriving on his horse, Otis, boots shit-caked—he'd been mucking the new stables near Thirty-Fourth. And soon after, Bernice Stilton, Dr. Constantine close behind: she couldn't get a cab in the drizzle.*

_____

*Bernice Stilton had called Dr. Constantine on the unlisted number Constantine keeps with the hope of hearing from Ariel, time zones and whatnot, New Zealand impossible; the number only to be used in emergencies. Constantine answered—she had been sleeping over Vicram's XXI, the chapter on the musings of his first wife, a woman who had agreed to free love, veganism, and meditation, and lived duly with it all until her untimely death from TB. "Hullo?" she said.

"Bernice," Bernice said.

"Bernice?" Dr. Constantine said.

"Listen," Bernice said. "I've made a mistake. I gave the keys to Elizabeth Fanning, Ben Hewitt's mom. She convinced me she needed something but I've got a funny feeling."

"Where is she?"

"At school, I presume," Bernice said.

"I'm on my way—"

"Be careful," Bernice says.

"Is she armed?" Dr. Constantine said, a joke.

"Not sure," Bernice said, humorless. "I'll meet you there."

Not for nothing does Bernice Stilton live in Penn South with the other ladies from the Garment Union days; not for nothing did she meet Rudy Stilton on a picket line, did they name their first son Lenin, did she carry the card from the Communist Party. Not for nothing does she sometimes wake to hear the thwack thwack thwack of the helicopters that dangle over Chelsea at odd hours, helicopters pursuing something—terrorists?—through the dark. She happens to know they've housed Homeland Security not too far west from here, in the old thread factory on Eleventh, the one where they

"Bernice," Elizabeth says. "Could you please tell him I'm a parent?"

"She's a parent," Bernice says. "What happened?"

"Nothing I can ascertain," Carlos says. "I found her here with a flashlight. She was on the stairs. She was heading up the stairs with a flashlight."

"I was on my way to the art room," Elizabeth says.

"The art room's on the third floor," Bernice says, helpful. "That makes sense," she says, as Constantine arrives.

"Who are you?" Carlos asks Constantine.

"I'm the head," Constantine says.

"And I'm the assistant head," Bernice says. "The keys are mine. My responsibility. She said it was an emergency."

"What emergency?" Carlos asks Elizabeth.

Elizabeth shrugs. "That's the thing," she says.

"She's a mother," Dr. Constantine says to Carlos, as if this explains everything. "I can vouch she's a mother," she says. She would rather just forget it, Elizabeth clearly out of sorts, maybe even a little unstable. Anyway, she does not want to see Progressive's name sullied and things too easily fall apart: there was the time the four-year-old, Belle, pushed her way out the unmanned door—since alarmed—with her best friend, Lolly, the two—it was cute, actually—heading to Lolly's apartment on West Tenth.

Carlos looks at the three women and then pulls the thick pad of paper from one of his many pockets.

Waste of time. False alarm, he does not write. He goes through the motions, signs his name, and notes the hour as Dr.

---

broke all the windows during Stonewall and looted in the Blackout of '77 and now, revamped, its skin a photovoltaic green, the Feds have taken over three whole floors, just above Fox News and under Scorsese.

Constantine and Bernice return to report nothing out of place but a miracle of the order they should all come see.

"Me, too?" Elizabeth says. She has been sitting in the dark window well, beneath the stitched-together quilt of the Class of '79. They had almost forgotten her.*

"You, too," Dr. Constantine says. And they follow her to the second floor, to K203, where the red glow of an incubator pulses in the corner, like an isolated heart, five newly hatched goslings asleep in a furry pile, their tiny beaks tucked under their tiny, tiny wings.†

---------------------

*Was this it, then? Her sense of slowly disappearing? Like in that cartoon she watched as a little girl where the character dissolved not all at once but as if someone were taking an eraser, wiping her away? Could she start again? Could she forget what she had done? Could she ever, even here, be forgiven who she was?

†Rebecca Hollingsworth had brought the eggs from the country last week, believing the project might boost her daughter Claudia's standing among the clique of girls who, in no small measure, have spent the past months excluding Claudia Hollingsworth from every game they invent in the playground— Mommies and Babies, Cops and Robbers, Blondes and Brunettes. Claudia doesn't appear to mind though Rebecca knows better. Or, rather, Rebecca minds. She has made up excuses to be there, to watch; Claudia sitting alone on the top of the monkey bars, talking to no one or to one of her imaginary friends. These times Claudia knows full well that her mother watches and so sprouts a pair of wings and lifts off from the monkey bars high over the City to observe the complexities of the traffic and the fascinating construction projects: the trucks, the jackhammers, the yellow and orange cones. Her imaginary friends suggest farther places, maybe returning to her country house to snuggle at the end of her bed, where it is always warm, and quiet, or possibly her grandmother's farm in Canada, but Claudia says no, she needs to be back for Snack.

Last week Rebecca had appeared at the door to K203, Ms. Greene's kindergarten class, citing the absence of nature from children's experiences in

"Beautiful," Carlos says.

"Yes," Dr. Constantine says.

His little girl had been in one of those incubators, Carlos says. Betsy. Born at twenty-six weeks with lungs too weak and small, the doctor said, he and his wife not even able to touch her, not even with the glove because she was hooked up to tubes. His wife was afraid she might jostle something and so she did not touch her and he did not and sometimes they wondered whether, you know, with the articles you see about bonding and so forth, they wondered whether they might have really screwed something up but their little girl fine now, a soccer player, a fourth grader but also so tough that they sometimes wondered. Margaret said she had a doctorate in education and please. She said, Please do me a favor and tell your wife not to worry. Please tell her not to worry.

They stand looking down at the goslings. Carlos asks permission and reaches into the incubator to lift the smallest one, the runt Claudia will be allowed to keep in the country, the runt she will name Pickles, its down still shell-stuck. Carlos holds it in his big hand, the runt settling down quickly, snuggling there tucked under the policeman's thumb as if the policeman were its mother.

---

the City, recent public scandals and school shootings elsewhere, the culture in general and commercialization in particular, carting the incubator, and the eggs the students might hatch as an experiment in *kinder* living, *kinder* a word, she would tell Ms. Greene and anyone else in the administration cornered to hear, that should be invoked more often, especially here, at Progressive K–8, a school on the forefront. And for that morning Rebecca had watched as her plan worked perfectly, as the other little girls—so kind!—gathered around her Claudia, touching her, hugging her, jumping up and down, laughing as Claudia beamed out from within them, from her place, suddenly, at the center of this world.

\*        \*        \*

"A misunderstanding," Margaret Constantine concludes.

"Don't do it again," Carlos says.

"I won't," Elizabeth says. "Temporary insanity," she says. "Honestly, I promise. I don't know what I was thinking."

They push open the heavy doors and walk down the steps of Progressive K–8 to the street, where Otis waits. The rain has let up, the City's lights softer somehow, exhausted as a child after a good cry.

Elizabeth pets the soft fur on Otis's neck, remembering how, when she was a young girl, a horse seemed the closest thing to heaven.

"Why Otis?" she asks.

"A dog I had once. An ugly bulldog."

"Oh," Elizabeth says.

She realizes they are all waiting for her to move along, to do something, to be okay. She should go home. The thing is, she should go home. She had only wanted to read again the other stories, the stories of the women who have met the deadline early. Insane, they might say of their schedules. Busy, busy, they say. I don't have a minute, they say. And still, It's all good, they say. We're fine.

"Best of luck to your son," Carlos says. He mounts Otis, who shifts his weight and keeps chewing. Carlos's raincoat, a duster, looks a cape in a different century.

"And to your little girl," she says.

Carlos waves good-bye to Margaret and tips his policeman's hat to Bernice. She blushes beneath the big frames of her plastic glasses and strokes the keys now safely tucked in her hand.

\*          \*          \*

Elizabeth apologizes to Constantine and Bernice again—but they'll talk about everything in the morning, Margaret says sternly.

She and Bernice wait, watching as Elizabeth rides her bike safely into the shiny, wet landscape, the random pulse of brake lights. Then the two, colleagues in a distant hierarchy, retire to one of the corner bars of the City often overlooked and for good reason. Screens hang like nattering stars in the dark and men slip from their barstools to form watery blurs that puddle and spread on the wooden floor.\*

"I don't know what's wrong with these women," Margaret begins.

"Hysteria," Bernice says. She ordered bourbon on the rocks with a twist to Margaret's martini, and it did not take them long to be on their second. "They're all hysterics. Just like the old days."

"I don't think so," Margaret says. "I was there in the old days."

"Anxiety then," Bernice says. "The curse of the twenty-first century." She would like to bum a cigarette off someone but remembers no one is allowed to smoke. Maybe that's the problem now: everyone needs a cigarette.

"Who knows," Margaret says.

"Not me," Bernice says. "But I've been at Progressive a long, long time and I've never seen anything like it. You would think they're all lining up to win the Nobel Prize. You would think the

---

\*A hundred years ago, sawdust and blood, but now just the smell of grease and the bang and clash of dishes washed too quickly by men paid too little. In her day, a June one in 1954, Bernice would have gone in back to ask them what, exactly, they earned. She would have wanted to practice her Spanish. But she's grown tired of Labor, she's grown tired of all that.

sun rises and sets on New York City. What more can they do? And this is what they get: loony tunes. I say, relax. I say it's all too much. I say, enough." She doesn't quite know what she says, actually, but it feels good to be gossiping with the boss, to be sitting directly across from the famous Margaret Constantine, PhD, heir to the throne, or at least for the time being, author of a number of papers concerning primary education and blah-da-de-blah. They run together now, all the Margarets and Steves and Carls and Veronicas—this a place where the heads don't stay too long before they roll out the door. Like the French Revolution. She would like to see Margaret's head roll out the door or she would not. Truly. Margaret a much nicer person than anyone would think. Here in the dark of the bar Margaret almost kind. Her boss had gone through the drill pretty quickly: the reasons Bernice should be fired, the reasons she would not fire her.

And then Margaret Constantine tells the bartender to put it on a tab.

And then she says to Bernice, Let's have another.

And then she says to Bernice, So, I understand you are not just the brains, but also the balls behind this entire operation.

But before any of it, Constantine turns to Bernice, Elizabeth disappearing into the shiny, wet landscape, and says, "I need a drink."


"We were in Scotland, a graduation trip. I must have said something terrible but for the life of me, I don't remember what. It hasn't been the same since."

In the dark, her boss looks almost pretty. She is pretty, actually. Bernice never noticed.

"Anyway, that's that. You? You've never said."

"You should call her," Bernice says.

"Who?"

"Ariel."

"I never know what time it is in New Zealand. I try to figure it out sometimes, just to see if she's brushing her teeth for bed or for morning. Just to picture where she might be standing."

"You could Google Earth."

"Maybe."

"You could zoom in. It's easy," Bernice says. She tells Margaret about her recent visit to Chita Goldman's first-grade class. Chita Goldman was showing the kids how to Google Earth on the Smart Board and used her own apartment—rent-controlled!— in the Bronx as an example of a location on Earth.*

"I suppose I could," Dr. Constantine is saying.

"What?" Bernice says; she's lost the thread.

"Google Earth," Margaret says.

"Right," Bernice says.

"And you?" Margaret says. "Children?"

"Two boys," Bernice says. "Dylan lives in Palo Alto. My oldest, Lenin, passed in 2004."

Iraq, she says, the irony. Lenin recruited from the hallways

---

*The kids sat in their kid chairs at their kid tables watching as Chita Goldman Google Earthed her apartment building in the Bronx, as she zoomed in—thirty-six years!—to show them a bird's-eye view of its brick façade, nothing special, and the seventh-floor window that would lead to her living room and the faded rose pattern of Chita Goldman's couch—it belonged to Nanna! If they could have gone in, and Chita Goldman explained that very soon they would be able to go in, given the advances of technology, drones the size of bees, pretty soon, Chita Goldman said, they would be able to go all the way into her apartment, to see the way she had left her dirty breakfast dishes on the red-checked tablecloth in the kitchen, to see her powder room with its windmill wallpaper, and the flowers in the vase in her bedroom, the kids now dead quiet as Chita Goldman went on, as she talked them through her entire apartment.

of PS 124, a crappy school then and more so now—this before
she organized Progressive K–8's employees to strike for a better family education policy. Every year they invite her back
for Veterans Day, she says. The commemorative reading of the
names the children painted on a mural outside the gymnasium,
a mural of doves and daisies and blue skies that has seen better
days and still, she goes. She returns to the crappy school to see
her boy's name among the other names and to greet the little
girls and boys who walk the line of now only mothers, shaking
hands and thanking them for their sacrifice.

There's a game on—basketball, some kind of rivalry that
has the mostly men at the bar suddenly cheering, a point won
or lost, fairly or unfairly, the referee a total dick, somebody's
shouting, a total, fucking dick.

"My sacrifice?" Bernice Stilton says, then nothing.*

---

*Carlos rides away in the rain, shamed for all he did not say about the
ugly bulldog, Otis. He could have told those women much more: How
Otis would ride shotgun, his paws on the dashboard looking out, and
how Otis's eyes were black, and how Otis smelled of his wife's powders
tucked as Otis often was within the covers of their bed. How Otis was
the first to rise and how Otis sometimes slept on his back, legs in the air
like an overturned bug, his wife would say, pointing and laughing, never
failing to be amused. How holding Otis he had watched the vet prepare
whatever it was and prime the syringe and how he wished his wife were
with him but she was not, this happening much too suddenly, this failure
of something vital, Otis unable to stand, unable to eat, Otis's black eyes
wrong, as if trapped behind scratched glass.

He'd cradled Otis in his winter coat to where the vet lived, the vet unable
to make it to the vet hospital but he would meet him in the vestibule and let
him up to his apartment. Carlos remembers all this in the reflective light of
the post-rain City, riding a bit distractedly up the bike path along the West
Side Highway toward the stables, the joggers and pedestrians and bicyclists
mostly inside due to weather except a few, a certain few, and so Carlos might

Margaret Constantine gestures to the harried bartender for the check, understanding that in the morning, or later in the morning, she and Bernice will meet again in the hallway outside of the administrative offices of Progressive K–8, where she will review her day's schedule, asking her if she might do a little rearranging given the late night. But now, it seems, they are friends, good friends, sailors on the same choppy sea; they push away from the bar and stand a bit unsteadily. From here they negotiate the dark to the door out, their beacon the red neon in the windows. From the west, Eleventh Avenue or maybe farther, a sudden eruption of sirens deafens everything, another emergency passing, almost gone; they stand on the sidewalk, waiting it out.

---

be forgiven for not calling backup for the furious bicyclist, the bicyclist's bicycle of the thousands of dollars variety now dented and thrown to the cement bike path, the bicyclist so furious he cannot speak. He shoves the person who has slowed him down, a young boy crossing the path to the river in search of something he cannot find elsewhere, something more than this, the bicyclist shoving the young boy against the cement barricades intended for suicide bombers, the young boy defending himself against the bicyclist and the policeman suddenly in the picture, a rookie who charges in alone, jumping off his horse to break it up. The switchblade intended for the bicyclist's neck lodged in the policeman's neck instead.

His blood was wet as the rain, the young boy would remember, will remember; the policeman's blood staining the cement barricade red so that many years later, many years passed, the young boy, now an ex–con artist, will spill the red paint on the cement gallery floor, bleached for this occasion—the occasion of the artist—prepared and prepped, the announcements mailed, the party planned, the ex–con artist at work on the installation, etching the flowers in the red paint with his fingers, the petals, the details he's known for—he's done this before—as he remembers the dead policeman, as he never forgets the dead policeman, the rookie, or the look of his dumb horse still waiting in the rain.

# XXI

Debussy's enchantment with the story of the sunken cathedral may have come from his summers in Brittany, near the Bay of Douarnenez, Helen's father said. A lovely place known for the sea and for the legend of the lost City of Ys (and here Helen, still a child, wonders if there are other magical cities named after letters of the alphabet: the City of Bs, the City of Xs), a city built out of the sea and circled by a high dike to protect it from tempests—rough storms, her father said. They say its only entry was an elaborate brass door on which artisans who had sailed down from the north had carved mermaids and mermen, the creatures' webbed hands and scaled tails worn from the many kisses of the king's admirers. The king, Gradlon, was a good king and had many admirers. Only he was good enough to hold the key to the famous brass door.

King Gradlon had one daughter, Dahut. The queen, his wife and the girl's poor mother, had died (and here Helen frowned; she did not understand why all the mothers in these stories had

to die when her own mother was in the kitchen frying meat-
balls in the electric skillet and perfectly alive).

The daughter, Dahut, was not quite as wonderful as her father.
In fact, she was terribly evil. She invited strangers into the city,
men whom she promised she would marry at dawn but whom
she killed instead at midnight. (And here Helen pictured her
mother, Louise, promising to marry her father, the moon high
over them, her mother, Louise, in one of her beautiful dresses,
and then . . . But she could not picture it. She could not picture
her mother as the evil Dahut, and anyway, her mother was calling
them. Dinner, she called.)

Anyway, the evil Dahut stole the key one evening for the
devil, her father says. (The devil!) And the devil unlocked the
brass door in the middle of a tempest and the waters rose and
drowned the city and Gradlon tried to escape on his magic
horse with Dahut behind him—

"Where?"

—on the horse but the Queen of the North—

"Who?"

I don't remember who. Someone appeared and said that
Gradlon must cast Dahut into the ocean.

"Her father?"

Yes. And so he did. And so she became a golden mermaid.

"On the brass door?"

In the ocean.

"Oh."

But the story is not what was important to Debussy. It was
what the story must have made him feel, her father says. There
is a difference, he says. Debussy's "The Sunken Cathedral" is the
musical version of Impressionism.

Had she heard of Impressionism? he asked.

"Of course!" she said. "Impressionism is when you shake the

hand of your teacher, or your friend's parents, before you are even asked."

You are a very smart girl, her father said.

You are the smartest girl in the room, her father said.

She does not move from her place on her father's lap even though he says Mother will be furious if the dinner gets cold. They cannot let Mother be furious, he says. Tonight they cannot let the dinner go cold, he says.*

She sat on her father's lap as her father told her the story of the music he played on the console, the brown furry thing in the corner Mother called his beast, his favorite animal. He explained how the story of the drowned City of Ys was a story that had been told over and over again by many different writers and artists and here a composer, so this was just one interpretation of a legend.

---

*Her father wears a small gray hat he takes off in church and when he walks through the front door home from work in his suit and tie. Where he works she is not sure: in an office in town, in a building cut from stone with a clock tower that counts every hour. He loves music the most, the piano; he loves the sound of the clock tower. He loves Mother, who sometimes dresses up to meet him in town, at Whitfield's on the corner, for lunch, and on those days she doesn't smell like Mother but like perfume. Today Mother met Father at Whitfield's and she watched as they walked up the walk to home, her mother pretty and her father handsome in his suit and hat. She dressed, too, in a starched dress that only yesterday hung on the line in the sunshine. She likes to picture her clothes there—on the line. Breathing the sunshine. She also likes to picture the fairies that live in the woods in the hollowed-out rotten tree trunk across Jackson's Creek, and in the moss that grows on its bark. The fairies plant tiny gardens there in rows and if you are quick enough you might catch them picking flowers but she has straight bangs that fringe her eyelashes and tickle and it is difficult for her to catch anything or even to see clearly. Still, she might with looking hard; her father always tells her to look hard.

Do you know the word *interpretation?* he said, and she said, "Of course."

Hold on, her father said.

He picked up the telephone from the small table next to his chair and her heart slipped believing he might change his mind and return to work after all, so late in the day, a spring day, the grass already green and birds singing in the trees and Mother in the kitchen in a pretty dress, believing maybe he will say into the big mouthpiece in the voice he used for work that he would head out after supper as he sometimes did, that he would be there soon. She watched her father listening as if the telephone had actually rung first. Did it ring first?

Then her father said, "Uh-huh." Then her father said, "I certainly understand, Mr. President. I will pass that along."

Her father set down the telephone and sighed.

"Well," he said to her. "You won't believe who that was: General Dwight D. Eisenhower. President of the United States of America."

"I know," Helen said.

"You do?" her father said. "And do you know why he was calling?" he said.

Helen shook her head quickly, a lie.

"Well," her father said. "I'll tell you why President General Dwight D. Eisenhower just rang me up," he said, peering at his daughter's eyes, huge behind the fringe of bangs his wife thought stylish, something to liven up a dull face, she said.

"He wanted to correct me," her father whispered. "'Not the smartest girl in the room,' Ike Eisenhower, thirty-fourth President of the United States of America, just said to me from his desk in the Oval Office of the White House. 'But the smartest girl on the entire planet!'" And here her father smiled his smile, his eyes bright behind his thick glasses, so much like her own in high school, where she sits in the darkened room looking at the slides of Matisse's blue dancers, her breath stopped in her throat.

This is what she remembered of the story "The Sunken Cathedral," Helen would say, if Sid Morris, or any of them, ever asked her inspiration.

# XXII

The movie star stands at his expansive kitchen window, wondering if he should have taken the architect's advice and knocked the brick wall open so the entire thing, the whole room, would be exposed to the back gardens of Chelsea. What the hell do you care, the architect had said. Everyone knows your business.

He had come to hate the architect, the way the architect rolled out his plans with a little snap, his starched shirt-sleeves neatly cuffed just below his elbows, his nails buffed. The architect would show him the various schemes he had worked through (on my dime, the movie star never added) before rejecting them for whatever the architect had singularly decided upon, what he would then argue for, invoking Corbusier, Kahn, even Wright, as if a Chelsea brownstone could rival Fallingwater, or that beautiful museum in Texas where once, a thousand years ago, the movie star had wandered unseen, unknown. He had been a student then, not a movie star. He had heard the famous professor's lecture on Kahn's genius in the famous class and watched as the large man stood on the stage of the lecture hall, the stained-glass windows bathing him in colored light, this a Gothic place, a vaulted place. The famous professor wept when he got to the part about Kahn's death alone in a bathroom stall in Pennsylvania Station, pants around his knees. The Last Crap lecture, the students called it.

The movie star had wandered in the art museum thinking of the famous professor and his lecture on Kahn, noting the architecture more than the exhibition, the way the light sluiced through narrow windows set somehow behind the angle of the walls, hidden yet emitting the light.

He had told the architect this when first meeting him, the architect a friend of a friend. Everyone always knew someone. The architect had also heard the Last Crap lecture, though a different year, and the two laughed at the famous professor, dead, one of them knew, a few years back. They walked through the brownstone, beginning in the dirt-floor basement and ending on the roof, where, the architect had said, if one had the right imagination (and a whole lot of cash, thought the movie star) one could build another story, maybe two: a hideout, a meditation room, a room of one's own. The brownstone hadn't been touched in sixty years. The possibilities were endless given the right vision, the right imagination, the right et cetera and whatnot (and buckets of cash, thought the movie star). They looked out. The sycamores and white pears that lined the street, the red brick of the seminary, its bell tower and bell that still tolled, on the hour, the cathedral and the beautiful gardens, closed most days to the public since 9/11 and now the site of the soon to be Desmond Tutu Inn and Suites; behind, in the back, the small gardens of the Chelsea brownstones and tenements—some just dog runs, others planted, each a tiny terrarium of hope—this one crisscrossed by Tibetan prayer flags, that one with all the wind chimes and birdbaths.

On one of his earlier visits to the house, the movie star felt

moved to tell the architect, he had watched as a hawk landed in
that giant mulberry a few gardens down. It had perched on the
top branch, camouflaged in the green, a rat in its talons it slowly
tore to pieces.

Impressive, the architect said, and it might have been then
that the movie star had begun to doubt him.*

Most people in the neighborhood recognized him immediately, though the neighborhood had, over the last decade,
become the kind of neighborhood where people were used to
seeing someone they had already seen ten times their original
size on a billboard or the side of a bus or a screen of one sort
or another. The people did their part: they did not stare as they
ate their red velvet cupcakes, sitting on one of the benches outside the famous cupcake bakery, or their organic ice creams on
their way up the steps to walk the High Line, where, inevitably,
they waited their turn to look through the telescope out at an
installation that meant something they waited in line to read
what. If they saw the movie star they walked on, or ground their
cigarettes into the sidewalk, or finished the dregs of their coffee
looking back at him as he looked at them: blankly.

And who was he, the movie star? A boy whose father took
the suitcase down from the hallway closet and buckled its straps,
a boy whose father took his hat from the top of the hallway
closet and put it on his head. They were in Georgia, or Louisi-

---

*The reason the movie star found himself in this house at all had to do with
divorce and custody, with bad breaks and unbelievable luck, a story the
tabloids distorted in the recounting—the movie star's ex-wife looking forlorn
even though she was the one to give him the boot, her modeling career as
meteoric, her face as famous as his and maybe even more so. She had tact-
fully kept to no comment and he had done the same. They were not the kind
of couple to sell photographs of their firstborn to magazines.

ana, somewhere warm, and outside the daylilies still bloomed and chameleons were black and just beyond, in the bayou, a cottonmouth swallowed a mouse whole. He saw none of it, the boy: he only saw his father leaving as his mother had asked his father to do, only saw the tips of his own filthy sneakers as he sat on the stairs and heard the screen door shut-slam on his father's way out. His mother said nothing as she sat in the living room waiting for his father to be gone. His father drove to the motel where later the boy would visit and wonder out loud what his father would next do.

"I don't know," his father had said. "I have no idea," the movie star remembers his father saying as he stands unseen in his Chelsea brownstone, his second wife out with the twins somewhere, in the park with the stone seals, he thinks she said. The swings if he was interested in joining them.

# XXIII

The waiter wipes their table with his dirty rag. He was Simone's favorite, Marie remembers: the son, Milo, with his bitten nails and his moods: he had a story to tell, Simone would say.

On the walls the Aegean coast in plastic frames and rows of photographs of models and politicians and actors in black and white, standing with Milo's uncle, John, or Milo's father, Demetrios, elegant, illegible signatures scrawled across their faces. Milo's father works in the kitchen. John's wife rings the register. The plate-glass walls look out to the corner of Ninth and Twenty-Third and the women watch as other women, other men, cross the avenue or wait to cross the avenue, the younger women in shorter skirts, Barbara's read, spring fashion. Umbrellas unfurled against the rain though they are useless, umbrellas; the enemy now the weather, someone says.

The skirts have always been above the knee, Franny says.

So, so above? Barbara says. There's a dot of mayonnaise on her lower lip no one bothers to point out. Her neck sags and a thousand years ago, Marie remembers, Barbara gave Simone

quite a run for her money. Oh well. Simone's dead and now
Barbara's neck sags like a turkey's and here they are, sleepless
and still not exhausted: everyone raring to go when the party
is almost over.*

---

*Sometimes, before, it had felt like they were in a boat, Marie and Simone,
Barbara, Donna, Franny, and all the others. More and more friends disappeared. The illness turned Bev Garfield's face to stone. Ida Pierce lost her
mind, first forgetting the word for sugar. Sugar, they had said to her, waving
the little white packets. *Sugar*. Trudy, whom they had loved, could no longer
walk, and so they had pushed her through the streets of Chelsea, down the
pitted, then-filthy sidewalks, struggling to smooth her way up over the frozen
curb and then steady again. They did what they had sworn they would never
do: they spoke of their health, they complained of aches and pains. They
couldn't go anywhere fast enough. "Come on," Trudy would say. "For the
love of God, push!"

In their boat the sea turned blue and black and gray; rocked and jos-
tled and crowded in, they were bored though sometimes not bored at all,
sometimes someone would tell a story and they would laugh until they
had tears in their eyes. They knew the story by heart, and still they would
laugh and wipe their eyes with their hands, strangers' hands, the skin
there, the bruises from their too-thin blood, the liver spots, the freckles,
their hands mosaics though that made them something else—art—and
they were flesh and blood, too. They still were flesh and blood. They stared
at their hands. They breathed. They slept. They stood from time to time
and stretched. It was eternal, the trip, though they were moving so slowly
they might have been going nowhere. Where were they now? Where had
they been? More and more Marie saw her family, her other one, far, far
away. She could see them but she could not reach them and besides if
she breathed, if she said one word, they would disappear. More and more
she smelled the apricot smell that sickened her: squashed black fruit, and
more and more she heard the loud buzz of bees—there were still bees,
impossible; fruit; her mother, her father, her sisters, her brother.

She climbs down, her body stiff from hiding. In other houses lights are
bright in the bluing dark. She smells the fresh dirt smell not so far from

here where other families live; she smells the sick sweet of apricots, feels the soft, rotten fruit on her bare feet. She smells her cold hands, her stink: onions, horseshit, fear. Someone pulls aside the draperies of St. Claire's Rectory, second floor, and stares out unseen. The Garmands' weather vane, a brass pig, looks a shadow: late spring and the days longer though still cold, the smell tire, ash.

Her mother's black shawl hangs on the nail behind the door, her sisters' work boots, mud-caked, beneath it, as if a body might get warm, dry. The fire is out. She sees her brother has left his spectacles on the kitchen table beside her father's books. Her brother might have been reading. Or he might have been roughhousing, her mother shushing him to quiet. At least remove your spectacles, she would say, *spectacles* a word she liked to speak out loud, the poetry of it, she said, the word as round as the thing, no? If you listen close everything's a poem, she had said.

But just last month Paula Feist had enough. She could no longer hear and she could no longer taste. The chemo sizzled her buds, she said; everything for shit. For a while she seasoned her eggs, her Ensure, with green chili powder, a gift from her oldest hotshot daughter in Santa Fe, a daughter who cast small goats with long horns out of bronze. A daughter in the newspapers. It all meant something Paula Feist had long ago forgotten, something vaguely religious, or pagan, or animistic. Paula Feist's hotshot daughter sold the goats in a gallery on a road of galleries run by other hotshot daughters, women in brightly patterned outfits with turquoise jewelry. The last time Paula Feist went to visit she had thought that perhaps she might live there, too. She liked the other women; she liked their smells, their clothing, the way they had of calling one another sweetheart. She liked the look of the Sangre de Cristo Mountains, blood-red at sunset, or sunrise. She liked the whole thing, she told her daughter. The whole package.

Her daughter had smiled, wanly, Paula Feist said, and said, "No, Mom. I don't think it would be a good idea for you to live with me. Sorry."

They knew it all already and besides, it is not a story to be told again, not one of the stories that will make them laugh until they have tears in their eyes. Those stories they can hear a million times but this story they would rather not hear again. Paula Feist understands this by the way the other

Four hours, Franny is saying. Four hours' sleep is the most I get. I don't know when it starts to happen. Sixty? Sixty-five? It sneaks up, Franny says. She spears a fry with her fork, cuts her meat patty, and jabs the whole in catsup. "It sneaks up."

"I've read melatonin," Barbara says, because she's always reading. "Melatonin regulates."

"What was that old commercial?" this Jane, the listener. "Regulate, regulate, Metamucil helps you regulate," she sings, her voice an embarrassment.

Milo appears from nowhere to clear their plates, his black vest stained but otherwise impressive, his white shirt starched. Marie took him for forties but Simone said younger: this kind of work and so forth.

"Ladies," Milo says.

"And gentlemen," Barbara says.

"Dessert?" Milo says.

"Rice pudding?" They crane to see the revolving dessert case near the front door, its trays of cakes and pies, shellacked, fly-flecked, as if perhaps something new is in the mix.

"It's Wednesday," Milo says.

"I wanted the rice pudding," Franny says. "I had a craving."

Milo winks. "I'll check," he says. He gathers the menus, huge in their old hands, then disappears again as the busboy descends to refill their waters.

"I'm going to float out to sea," Franny says, watching him.

---

women shift in their seats, looking out to the frothy waves, white-capped, ominous. The sky darkens, the sun filters through in brilliant shafts of copper and pink. They remember it well, the sun, remember how Paula Feist chose this day to climb out, the way her old legs seemed young, again, the way her arms pumped to push her forward.

Or maybe the boat has always been empty.

"Milo's looking haggard," Barbara says, though no one's paying much attention. They stare out the plate-glass windows thinking of this and that—someone has painted a sprig of holly on the glass for Christmas but it's spring, already. In the community garden folks are planting peas and uptown, Donna says, in Central Park, the daffodils have started blooming in those great glorious waves, hundreds of them, thousands, and those trees they have the children shouldn't climb. She'd been there with her grandson, Atlas—who thinks of these names?—and the security had come and said don't climb and Atlas's mother, you remember Jenny, no shrinking violet, had said she'd climbed those trees when she was a little girl and what the fuck?

She said that?

To the guy's face.

"Not since 9/11 do they let you climb trees," Barbara says. She read it.

No.

Atlas.

Atlas.

So Atlas was grounded.

Donna takes a sip. "Atlas was pissed," she says.

Outside a siren then a fire truck and then another and then another; a line of police cars follow.

"Someone's climbing trees," Barbara says.

"It's a Surge," Marie says. She watches the long line of police cars and fire trucks and motorcycles framed in sprigs of flaking holly or possibly mistletoe through the glass, all the vehicle lights going but no sound at all; the sound nothing, quiet as the quiet before All Clear.*

---

*Thirteen and a stale bun in her hand, cold cup of tea—they believed her seventeen and she let them, she at her desk filing or mimeographing—

"All thanks to Mr. Kelly," Franny says.

"Gene?"

"Hah! I wish!" she says.

"I can still remember my first Surge," Barbara says. "New York. Nineteen sixty-seven."

"That wasn't a Surge that was a Police Action. I was there. The gays, right?"

---

would it have been mimeographing? Always a quick study. Purple ink on her fingertips, her raggedy nails she bit when she couldn't find a cigarette. The machines they used. Bulky monsters. The sounds of the tick-ticking, or the thunk, or the whiz. You listened for the sounds and it would always be her luck to get in line behind Bramwell, greasy-haired married man she had tried to avoid: him with his wife and children in Cheshire waiting it all out.

If there weren't no war he would've made one to send the wife away, Shirley said. Shirley of Camberley-Frimley—like a bad limerick, Abe said—and the London flat they shared with its broken heat box and wet walls and blackened windows and the little potted plant Shirley called Alice and the poor goldfish with no name she called No Name that swam around and around in the hazy water of its glass bowl. She told Abe once about it; she told Abe once about everything and then she did not ever again: Shirley with her black-inked eyes and shorn hair and tiny, elfin hands. She had had some sort of childhood illness that kept her small. She knitted socks and listened to the wireless with the rest of them, never hurrying, reluctant to go to the public shelter and then going as if only agreeing to dance with the last man because he was the last man. If I must, Shirley said, up from her chair and tucking her knitting into the wicker basket with the leather strap meant for fish. My father's, she told Marie: dead in the First. They went down the steps to the darkened room, the air dank, stuffy, listening to Jerry's offerings, praying someone had lit one of the oil drums nearby, praying for a night dark from burning oil but the nights were never dark; they were bright with fires, the stench as sharp in the morning as the blaring all clear. Shirley at Balham Station when the bomb ruptured the water main; Marie may have been there, too, but in the country that day with Alice. Take Alice, Shirley had said. She needs a little cheering up.

"Felt Surge-ish."

"Here I am like a chicken with my head cut off. Thought something had happened," this Donna.

"Nineteen sixty-seven," Franny says.

"Two thousand two," Donna says. "My first."

"That was anthrax," Franny says.

"And what about anthrax?" Barbara says. "Whatever happened to anthrax?"

But no one seems to know, the Surge endless, police car after police car after police car after fire truck after motorcycle after police car after police car after police car after police car, like a parade with no candy, no spectators, no high school beauties, cheerleaders, or flag twirlers. No one on the sidewalks paying much attention either except the tourists, who have no idea what could possibly be going on below—New York! They stand on the High Line looking down.

Should they run for their lives?

"Where to?" says the guy shaving gourmet shaved ice, kimchi or boysenberry, take your pick.

And back at the Galaxy, among the regulars, Milo appears with a tray of rice pudding. Five cool bowls of white in frosted glass, intended for Friday's rush, he says, but for certain customers like his favorite Chelsea ladies, Wednesday's the new Friday.

# XXIV

Helen is swept along in the rush of water at Great Falls, her mother's voice jerked away as quickly as the flip-flops yanked from her feet. She reaches for overhanging branches that have snagged other things but they snap in her hands and were never strong enough anyway. She cannot breathe.

She is drowning. If she opens her eyes she might see but she cannot open her eyes; they are painted shut. She imagines an empty boat, anchored and steady. She thinks hard of the anchored boat rushing toward wherever she is being rushed toward. It could also be a house, or a palace. It could be a cathedral. If she could open her eyes she would know if this were the dream again or if this were real but she cannot open her eyes. She can only feel the rush and the pull and the constancy of the water, the constancy of the constancy of the water in the dark.*

_____

*It was her father who had told her the story of the Cathedral of Ys, the legend Debussy had in mind when he wrote "The Sunken Cathedral," a legend from when languages were spoken that no longer are spoken, when legends stood in for history, he said: one and the same. He told her this story as he had told her the story of the Black Swan and the Remarkable Tailor because, he told her, he believed her to have a passionate soul, a soul that hangs back, watches, takes it all in: Think of deer bounding into a glade, he said. Some of them, most of them, know no better and leap in unaware—picture a meadow full of April wheat and wildflowers and everything else that would be delectable to the deer, hungry from a harsh winter. Who can blame them? But a few hang back, maybe one or two, waiting. They know that a man might stand in the shadows of the distant woods, his rifle poised. That at any moment they might hear the crack of gunshot, smell the spent metal smell though of course they don't know the words for these things, only the feelings. Those are the deer that will survive, her father said: the ones with the passionate souls, the feelings. The ones that look hard.

Do *you* have a passionate soul? she had asked him, and her father had thought about it for a moment before answering, Yes. I believe I do. Yes.

# XXV

There always remains the possibility that Progressive K–8 will be canceled due to inclement weather. It often is. sleet, snow, ice, wind. Last week the subways broke down again and the buses were stranded in pools of water on the east and west highways, water that rose and sloshed over the already battered guardrails, insurmountable flaws in the grading and infrastructure of everything. Chita Goldman, in Riverdale, watched it all on television, thinking not for the first time that her ancestors, fled here from Latvia, had it right to choose the Bronx. Higher ground, she thinks. Not like Far Rockaway. Or God forbid, Staten Island.

Now she sits at her seventh-floor window looking out at the rain that falls in torrents. No Hudson River light today, no more the subtle glow that inspired all those painters, that fell on the river at a certain time each day. The Palisades is a fortress of black and gray rock and here, in her neighborhood, the sycamores snap like twigs, the air alive with all the swirling leaves never raked from autumn. The first winds will be the strongest, the newscasters had said, though who believes them anymore? When it comes at last, when it *lands*, like a train crashing through an actual station, or a satellite dropped from the sky, a whoosh and a blow, a screeching hurl, Chita Goldman, given her lineage, given the hellholes her relatives survived and then some—on both sides—is not as afraid as she imagined she would be in the next disaster. She runs to shut her bathroom window tight against the driving rain, fastening the lock as if the rain were a thing with hands and will, wanting in.

# XXVI

"Do you want to know my Who We Are fantasy?" Elizabeth asks Pete. It is early morning of another week.*

---

*The truth is she *had* been on her way to the third floor, the art room—the papier-mâché sea creatures strung with dental floss from the orange-painted water pipes, Ben's a slow-turning, wonderpus octopus. He had loved those creatures once. She could still remember him insisting she nightly ask the questions—did they still exist? Yes. What did they eat? Other fish, crabs. Where did they live? The shallow waters of Indonesia and Malaysia. She was on her way to find brushes or, even, spray paint. She was going to write something, or draw. Something big. Something she had been meaning to remember forever—the way her Ben had once been a little boy, the way he had wanted to know if she, too, counted the wonderpus octopus among her favorites; and Molly, always Molly: Molly turning and waving with her mittened hand. Just that morning demonstrating how she could tie her laces the rabbit-ear way. And now, getting to the edge of the pond Elizabeth saw how Molly had already run onto the ice, the ice already cracking as she waved, happy, her shoelaces untied, both boots. But she said none of this to Carlos. Instead she told him how she had always liked the art room best. How things had been a little tense: her husband's job; a teenage son; time passing; the City.

You don't know the half of it, Carlos said. We're all in the same boat.

Are we? she said. We are?

"Us," she says to Pete. "What we have. I probably don't say it very often."

"Ever," he says.

"I probably don't say it ever," she says.

"Never," he says.

The sun in their bedroom they have agreed they will miss the most. The sun in their bedroom and the view of the sycamore branches from their bedroom window. The red-brick glow of the seminary at a certain time of day and the entire brownstone street, systematically purchased by a Russian billionaire who banks, rightly, on the neighborhood's property values given the construction of the High Line and Manhattan real estate in general: that they will not miss, or the influx of the British—why?—or the wail of the ambulances now crossing over for Bellevue.

"So maybe, Paris?" she had said. They were considering options of where to live next—the suburbs? "I could home-school Ben. Or Denmark. I'd be up for that. The happiest people live in Denmark. I read it somewhere. Did you read that? And Denmark has all those systems against the rain; they've got it figured out."

"I'm going to commute from Denmark?" he said.

"Maybe," she said. "You could do the transatlantic thing."

"And this," she says. "Where we are now. Who we are," she says.

"Okay," he says.

He looks tired.

"Okay," he says again, passing her on his way to the bathroom.*

---

*He is an eighteen-year-old boy walking his girlie pink bike next to her, following until he finally gets the nerve.

"Aren't you in Nietzsche?" he asks.

"Dostoyevsky," she says.

"Right," he says. *The Possessed.*

He is an eighteen-year-old boy who rolls his own cigarettes, a boy who camps in the boiler room too poor to pay the dorm fees. A sneak he was then and the janitor knew and the janitor kept a lookout for Maintenance or Grounds or anyone else coming around, promising to warn this poor boy he has taken such a shine to and in the meantime, he says, go ahead and stash the sleeping bag near the warm pipes. The janitor's name Poppy, he tells him—Poppy's real name too difficult to pronounce, French by way of Haiti, did the boy know Haiti?

Pete, Pete says.

Too many ghosts, Poppy says.

Poppy leans against his mop in the boiler room where he has found Pete in his sleeping bag, Pete oversleeping—he's usually already gone, the sleeping bag stashed on the landfill, between the rocks. Idiot he is, folding a shirt over his eyes to drown out the red exit lights and in the too-dark and warmth he's already missed two classes. This is a temporary arrangement, Pete says, and Poppy laughs, saying, "What's not a temporary arrangement?"

"Nothing, I guess," Pete says, rolling a cigarette, offering it to Poppy.

"Your age I worked in the hospital. Port-au-Prince. All day long sick people," Poppy says, flicking some tobacco off his lip, lighting the thin cigarette with a steady hand. "Wished I could go to school."

"I can imagine," Pete says.

Poppy cocks his head, stares straight at Pete, and blows.

"You can't imagine shit," he says, pinching the end of the cigarette and putting it in his shirt pocket.

"Sorry," Pete says, lighting his own.

"Against the rules," Poppy says.

"Sorry," Pete says.

"Have to make it known," Poppy says.

"I'll find somewhere else," Pete says.

"No smoking," Poppy says, then looks at Pete and laughs.

The next morning Poppy arrives before Pete has the chance to slip out—Poppy temporary, too, he tells Pete, until the Lord decides otherwise.

"Teach me," Poppy says, Poppy a quick learner, *Hop on Pop* his favorite—Pete waiting for his steady finger to move to the next word, trying not to say it aloud, his whole self crazy with wanting Poppy to say it aloud—he never wanted anything more than for Poppy to read this word and then the next, the whole sentence, to get on with it. And he did, Pete tells Elizabeth. He does, he says to Elizabeth. Lizzie in high school but since college Elizabeth.

Elizabeth, he said, as if it were a name difficult to pronounce.

Like wildfire, Pete says. The guy's obsessed.

They lie on the narrow single in Elizabeth's dorm room, a thin sheet over them, wet in certain places, the top sheet from the twin set with the scalloped yellow edge her mother insisted she bring with her to school, to remind her of home, her mother had said, in case you feel lonely.

The twin sheet went with the cartoon comforter, Tweety Bird and Sylvester. She pulled the comforter up to her chin now, wanting to be covered ankle to neck; they had classes but decided to stay in bed all day. Later they would get Chinese and beer and ride to the rocks where he'd stashed his sleeping bag before meeting Poppy. But before any of this, before meeting him, Pete was a boy who rode his pink girlie bicycle around campus. She would see him sometimes and then she would not, until one day she saw him everywhere. "Are you following me?" she said.

"Yes," he said.

"I thought so," she said.

"Aren't you in Nietzsche?" he said.

"Dostoyevsky. *The Possessed*."

"Close."

"Not really," she said. He wore a button-down plaid shirt with a frayed collar; she had on a fringed jacket, feathers dangling from her ears. He smelled of tobacco and needed a shave. Just that morning, Poppy had told him he looked like a bum.

He walked his ratty pink bicycle beside her and told her he had grown up outside Seattle, like nobody else there in the Midwest, and that he found the cold really cold and the wind almost unbearable and the whole windchill thing impossible to understand and she said, "We're talking about the weather?" and he said, "No, we're going to the Paramour." But it wasn't yet three and besides, she had things to do: she worked as a hostess at the

Pete walks back in from the bathroom and sits on the edge of the unmade bed tying his dress shoes; then he straightens up and looks at her, hamster trance.

"Early meeting?" she says.

"Yup," he says. "I'll check in later."

"Okay," she says.

---

Keg and she needed the cash and extra tips because she had blown a lot recently, literally, she said, but he didn't get it, and later, when he did, he convinced her not to bother, sex better without coke, like the old days, he told her. "Real old-time fucking," he said. "Like in the movies."

But before he said any of it, she said, "Carry me," and he did, Pete in front pedaling, riding the two of them double on his rickety bike, bought at a garage sale from a family in Winnetka, four children all grown and flown the coop, the father said, watching Pete pick through the bikes and the bins of his sons' and daughter's clothing, dressed for his later doubles game in white.

Youngest left just last week, he said. This is something we've promised ourselves.

Necessary, Pete said to the man, the father of four all already grown.

The man looked like a doubles player; he looked like a cheat. A lawyer downtown, he told Pete. You?

Philosophy, Pete said. I don't know. Haven't decided. Maybe philosophy.

Big decision, the man said.

I suppose, Pete said, then, choosing the pink, he said, This one.

Caroline's? the man said. Really?

Sure, Pete said, pulling bills from his pocket.

He had wanted to rock the man's world, Pete yelled, to shake up the doubles game, he yelled, and how is she doing back there? he yelled. She has heard some of what he said but not all; he has given her most of the seat and she holds tight to his waist, eyes closed, her head pressed against the warmth of his sweater, feeling the softness there, this the kind of sweater you might find at the bottom of a drawer or the back of a closet and wonder how long it had been lost to you, how you could possibly have survived without it; this the kind of boy you could love.

Behind him the old print from graduate school, bought at the Met or one of those stores in New Haven: Matisse's *The Conversation*, the husband standing and the wife sitting, looking up at him. The man, Matisse, hand in the pocket of his striped pajamas, the woman, his wife, Amélie, in a long black dress, her arms on the arms of the straight-backed chair. There is a beautiful garden through the window; there is a canvas of blue all around them. Maybe they have just wed; maybe they are long married. Maybe he's a saint; maybe she's an angel. Maybe he's a sonofabitch; maybe she's unfaithful. Still: here they are who they are: together.

# XXVII

On the steps of Progressive K–8, the seventh grade ethics class gathers for Survival, Ms. Kim clapping her hands and saying today is the day they've been waiting for, the day to practice Screams. A handful of faculty corral them into smaller groups, offering them advice—don't knock anyone down, don't run into the street, keep your wits about you, keep your pants on. The students head out, each to a different avenue, a different block, on their own, their shadow teacher shadowing them, waiting for the right moment.

Ben's crush, Esme Perkins, lingers outside the falafel place on Bedford when she feels the slithery hands reach around from behind, pulling her in, tightening their grip, the breath warm or even hot in her ear saying nothing. She panics, remembering absolutely nothing except the sound of her heart, doubled, and believing that these hands, this breath, are not the hands and breath of Ms. Collins, assigned as her shadow she happened to know—they had all seen the sheet—but rather the hands and breath of a criminal, a terrorist who will slip the noose around her neck and drag her away to be killed. Then she hears Ms. Collins's nice voice in her ear: "You're supposed to scream, Esme. You're supposed to run for your life."

And so she does. She screams. Esme Perkins, twelve years old
and only recently in proud possession of breast buds, her under-
pants etched with the days of the week and still insistent on
matching Sunday for Sunday, screams. She screams and screams,
twisting free from Ms. Collins's grip, not insubstantial given Ms.
Collins's, soon to be Mrs. Prandori's belief in the plank, which
she holds every morning for seven minutes and counting, aim-
ing to work up to ten before her June wedding to Reynolds
Prandori, a man she met in graduate school who still believes
her decision to teach science to seventh graders beneath Ms.
Collins's dignity. But how can she ever show him what? Even
here, watching Esme Perkins scream and flail as she runs down
Bedford toward the steps of Progressive K–8, Ms. Collins's heart
breaks a little, like a thin-shelled egg tapped with a knife. What
next for these children? What possibly next?

# XXVIII

The boxes obstruct the passage through the house, Larry and Jules arguing it best to put Great-Aunt Eleanor's valuables into immediate storage until they can get the right appraiser, someone they have used in the past in Los Angeles, to determine the value of the whole.

"There's shitloads to do," Marie's heard Larry say on the telephone. "A mountain of crap."

She's given them the front room, her room—the comfortable queen, Very Grand attending—and moved into the sitting room with the daybed Abe dragged home from the street, the streets full of bounty then, all the SROs converted at a clip so that entire wardrobes might be found on Twenty-Second, Twenty-Fourth, Nineteenth, armoires reeking of cat pee, their faux oak doors peeled or peeling, papered with stickers from various campaigns. Once a gramophone; once a set of rusting golf clubs though neither of them played; once a banker's box filled with postcards, letters, tax returns. Abe had said he couldn't stand to see it all there for anyone to read. He planned to use the shredder and do the job properly.

In the last three weeks Jules has hired his appraiser. He has hired a real estate agent. He has hired the painters. He has hired

the roofers. He has hired a maid. He has hired the liquor store
to deliver straight to the front door exactly what he wants since
Jules has become something of a wine connoisseur and Larry,
apparently, always was.*

Marie wanders among the boxes, making do with a cane,
the cast dirty, the symbols Sid Morris said meant something,
painted with his shaky hand in the colors best for healing,
grungy with wear, the heel filthy. Next week the doctor will
slice it off, Larry said. The cast! Larry said. Not the foot! He had
seen her expression. Things have suddenly become confusing; it
is difficult to negotiate the hallway with these boxes. She loses
track. The best thing, for the time being, sleep, Jules said. They
will do all that needs to be done, he said. They have flown home
and flown back in a little over a day. They have crisscrossed the
entire country and arrived again at her doorstep.

"You're here," she said, opening the door to them. Had they
been to the grocery? To the theater? A museum?

"We've been to California, Ma," Jules said, taking her hands.
His eyes are Abe's eyes; he is already older, tall and thin.

But she can no longer sleep, she could tell him. She no longer sleeps.

She stands in the kitchen at the back window, watching Roscoe balance on the high fence between the two backyards, his

---

*Marie heard something on the front stoop and stepped out. This is all she
says she can remember: robe, slippers, a cast, and crutches in the rain. It
was the middle of the night. Stroke of luck that crossing Ninth—toward the
seminary?—she met the tenant, Elizabeth, bicycling home. Elizabeth herself
quite undone, Jules said: maybe the weather or, God knows, that teenager.
We should all live on the West Coast, he said. Anyway, Elizabeth returned his
mother long after midnight. We're talking about a woman who would never
go anywhere without her face on, Jules said.

And only then had Marie agreed to sell.

tail quivering. It is early morning, earlier than that, and there are crickets already, the weather spiked. In virtually one day: spring. Perhaps tomorrow the cherry will bloom, perhaps the day after, Monday, or Tuesday. You can never tell: its blossoms a dull pink, slightly folded at the center, reluctant. The tree, grown tall as the brownstone, spreads out over the back garden, umbrellas it in spindly limbs and others broken at the joints—the weather. It is an ornamental species, complicated, fussy: its narrow trunk and branches, filly gray and slender, are similar to a fruit tree, an apricot, prone to blight and apple rust. But here again its leaves curl inward, a fist refusing to give up its treasure.

A soft knock.

"Elizabeth?" the voice familiar in her sleep, slightly accented.

Elizabeth's out of bed quickly, her jeans on the chair. "Coming," she calls. "I'll be right there," she says, and she is, the apartment tiny after all, just one narrow floor, a hallway with two small bedrooms and a bath between the street-facing living room and the garden-facing kitchen, the kitchen table centered on the back windows so she can sit here and see the view—the movie star's birch, the other neighbors' mulberry where once, last spring, she watched a hawk with a rat in its talons. Mrs. Frank has owned the brownstone for more than fifty years and raised her own boy here, she told her when they'd met that first day. A coincidence.

Destiny, Elizabeth had said.

Mrs. Frank had smiled, offering quiche and a glass of wine, her kitchen a beautiful yellow, her bedroom regal, a portrait— a distant relative, she'd said—above the carved mantel. The smell of that apartment, as she later told Pete, as if all of the things crowded there gave off a certain odor of, what? History? Life? The china and the gold, the tiny photographs framed in sil-

ver, the letter openers, the crystal, the wallpaper, the faux gas
sconces, the copper pans in the kitchen, the stewpots. Her husband had been a pack rat, Mrs. Frank said.

Wonderful, Elizabeth said, idiotic, but she had milk brain
and besides, she did find it wonderful. Anyway, she said. We'll
be quiet as mice.

I don't want mice, Mrs. Frank said. I want nice, she said. She
has the most amazing blue eyes, Elizabeth told Pete.

We're nice mice, Elizabeth said. She was delirious from lack
of sleep; her breasts ached and leaked. They needed another
room: a room for the baby, a room she might share with him, a
desk and a crib. And at first, she tried: she waked early mornings
and wrote: "The Story of Molly," she called it. It began like this:
There once was a little girl named Molly. But then she listened
to her baby breathe. She liked to listen to her baby breathe. Is
that weird? she asked Pete. I could listen to Ben breathe all day
long. Sometimes I just sit there and watch him breathe and then
I get all wiggy and think, If I walk out of this room, he will stop
breathing.

Morbid, Pete said.

Exactly, Elizabeth said, but it was true.

Then Elizabeth tried to write "The Story of Molly" in the
afternoons, between feedings, but there were no between feedings; the day the meal, the meal the day: Ben ravenous.

You're a writer? Mrs. Frank had asked.

Yes, Elizabeth had said, the quiche delicious. Well, I write
poetry. I mean, I wrote poetry. I can't really call myself a poet. I
haven't been published or anything.

You're a poet, Mrs. Frank had said.*

---

*Tiny! she had told Pete, like a French Audrey Hepburn but tinier than that
and the most incredible blue eyes.

\*      \*      \*

Elizabeth opens the door to Marie in housecoat and slippers, suddenly old. Perhaps she has come to apologize for that bit of business in the rain—they haven't seen each other since—or with the news Elizabeth has already heard from Jules, and before that from the boyfriend, Larry. It's only a matter of time, he had said. They had crossed paths on Eighth. We're on a reconnaissance mission: project Chelsea. Jules hates to do it but given everything, what else can be done?

I see, Elizabeth said.

The neighborhood is through the roof. You know, the High Line. Jules thinks we should strike while the iron is hot. Jesus, I'm cliché man.

Larry laughs, squinting at Elizabeth as if she is lit from behind. He clearly likes and does not like to be the deliverer of this news, although he seems a decent enough fellow, Elizabeth later tells Pete. He has the look of a Broadway dancer; she could picture him running up a lamppost singing something from *Oklahoma!* or *South Pacific.* He is handsome that way—

---

Wasn't she French? Pete said.

Who?

Audrey Hepburn, Pete said.

Dutch, I think. A war refugee. Malnourished. That's why she was always so thin.

But why speak of Audrey? she wanted to say to Pete. The point was Mrs. Frank: the look of the beautiful black-and-white photograph of the dead husband, Abraham Lincoln Frank, and the little boy Jules, Elizabeth had admired and all the other things on the ornate walnut sideboard, pennies in a bowl, etched glass, quills, and sundials. They'd had an espresso after their wine. They'd nibbled sugar cookies. It had all been something, she would say: miniature and beautiful and perfect. Like a lost fairy world.

the smoothest baby skin, a nice smell. Anyway, he says. It's all the same to me. I need to get back to California.

He worked for Legal Aid: total insanity, a billion cases on the docket. They want me to be a judge, eventually, so they're watching, you know, like everything I do. Usually you're on your own ticket. Deadlines.

Larry's eyes wander to a couple passing with a small dog on a leash. The couple waits as the dog hunches its hindquarters, shivering, shitting on the sidewalk.

Jesus, I still can't get used to that, Larry says, though they both watch as one of the men bends over to scoop up the dog mess with his bagged hand. Near him, on the railing intended to protect the tree trunk, a handmade sign asks all dog owners to curb their dogs. PLEASE LET ME GROW IN PEACE, it reads. NAMASTE.

"I want you to look at something," Marie is saying. "I need you to look at something." She limps by Elizabeth to the kitchen window facing the back, above the square of garden Marie still maintains—Elizabeth at odd times watching her as Marie putters about or sits in one of the rusting wrought-iron chairs.*

---

*A few months back Pete had said he was sure there was a man there, too. He said he heard a man's voice. "It's the movie star," she said. "He's always on his roof acting." But Pete said, no, a different man's voice, and look, he said. "Someone's down there."

"Do you think he's her suitor?" Pete whispered, and something about the way he whispered or maybe even said *suitor, suitor* a word like *blank* or *giggle,* made Elizabeth laugh and remember how much she loved him. She laughed and then she said, "God, I hope so," and pulled Pete down to crouch at the back window, where they could listen and spy and maybe it was Pete's idea or maybe it was hers but eventually Pete slid off her jeans on the kitchen floor in the way of years before so that she could not think

"Do you see?" Marie is saying. "Look!" And Elizabeth does; she looks to where Marie points: the cherry tree suddenly and remarkably in full bloom.

---

of anything but Mexico and the convent and the little bird that hopped off its perch to read her fortune. What had been her fortune? This? Here? But no, it had been something else entirely, hadn't it? She had no idea, she thought, losing whatever else she thought to nothing but the feel of him in her, with her.

# XXIX

W hat If your parents split when you are just a child?
What If the man you love loves men instead?
What If your child dies before you do?
What If your family disappears in an instant?
What If the plane goes down instead of up?
What If the boy refuses to say your name?
What If the man you love loves no one?
What If your brother does not leave a note?
What If your husband can no longer sleep?
What If your wife always leaves the room?
What If the ocean swamps the boat?
What If the forests burn?
What If the girl slips beneath the ice?

# XXX

It is both true, and banal, that sometimes who you are changes in an instant. This is how Elizabeth will eventually begin "The Story of Molly." She has come to understand the importance of structuring the details around a narrative, the expectation of histories having a beginning, a middle, and an end, though she doesn't really believe this is the way life works: she does not know the way life works. She will perhaps include the Mexican chairs and Pete's pink bicycle; Molly's mitten in the ice, found later frozen like an autumn leaf. The black ice killed her cousin, Molly. Fact. Elizabeth was in charge for the afternoon. Fact. The pond was forbidden. Fact.

Everyone said they forgave her. Accidents happen. Her aunt and uncle said it, too, after a while, after a few years, after her aunt howled in a way that Elizabeth had never heard a human being sound, in a way that she will never, ever, forget.

# XXXI

Helen finds the sunken cathedral at the bottom of the sea, tangled in dark seaweed, its windows crusted over with dull shells and patterns left from the anemones, the snails and sea urchins that have moved on, and though she is bruised and sore from her own drowning, from the tumult and the weight of the water, from the explosion of her lungs, she swims beautifully toward it, her hands grown webs, her legs fused. In time she might rise to the surface of the water to sit on a rock and wreak havoc with the sailors, but now there is no hurry, the sea suddenly peaceful, her mother's voice so distant as to no longer be heard above the chiming of the cathedral bells or maybe that's only the wind; it might be only the wind above; there is now only wind.

# XXXII

The movie star says he is beginning to forget who he is or, rather, who he was because he had been someone before and now it seems he is no one or, rather, he is only who others believe him to be. Everyone always believes him to be the person they think he is, which in truth is no one.

What do you mean? Slotnik asks.*

You know, not me but one of my characters, the movie star says.

He has been trying to understand himself, but every time he gets close to understanding, his mind wanders, as if bored. He is trying his best to explain it all to Slotnik, who, typically, jumps

---

*Slotnik asks although she believes she already knows. Slotnik believes there is very little she does not know; very little she has not heard before. She has been around so long she has come to think that she has listened to the demons of every artistic person of a certain means, and many others on a sliding pay scale, in lower Manhattan, which may be true, though the fact that she listens to both the movie star and his neighbor Elizabeth is pure coincidence, the kind of thing that often happens in New York City, though no one can explain why.

ahead to supply details that are both ridiculous and correct. This
Slotnik habit infuriates the movie star but is also the reason why
he is in Slotnik's office. Although he has seen numerous thera-
pists over the years, they run together as bland as paint mixed
from several pints, the color a dingy brown. Brown, he thinks
now, the color of therapy.

He pulls his mind back to the present, to the heavy, draped
room with its requisite African art and, inexplicably, poster
of Provence. On the coffee table, an odd collection of knick-
knacks—glass animals, mostly, elephants and camels and deer
and rabbits—march toward him. Bookshelves line the walls
crammed with volumes on the brain, on interpreting the
brain—the child's brain, the teenage brain, the brain on drugs,
the aging brain—even a few on the soul, though Slotnik has said
she believes the soul would be much better understood as the
self, a construct that resides between the heart and the stomach,
closer to the lungs, possibly, or wedged somewhere near a rib.

My mother had a floating rib, the movie star said. I never
understood it. She spent days on the couch.

Precisely, Slotnik said.

I always pictured it suspended inside of her—you know, kind
of floating there, sort of boomerangish or like the Starship *Enter-
prise*.

She was your universe, said Slotnik.

She's still alive, he reminded her.

She is your universe, said Slotnik.

She's her universe, the movie star said. That time he had
been in a feisty mood, eager to speak ill of his mother.*

---

*Abigail. Her name fitting her like one of the white gloves she and her
friends still wore to church, Presbyterian, gloves they removed and folded
and set next to them in the wooden pews, the empty fingers splayed on

Tell me, Slotnik said. She seemed interested.

Abigail still lived in the small town in Louisiana where the movie star had been born, a detail repeated quite often in the small town, so that now the signs that marked the town limits, both coming and going, include a rendering by a local artist of the movie star's silhouette, along with the movie star's name and birth date and the fact that, in addition to being a movie star, he had also been the winningest quarterback for the high school team, known then as the RedMen but now, due to a civil suit by the Muscogee in which the sensitivities of the Wild Snake rebellion were noted, known as the Men.

So it's a big deal, the movie star said. Me: who I am.

They were in their first session and the movie star felt, as he did whenever he attempted this business, that he needed to offer a thumbnail, or blueprint, for what she should know, since everything she might think she knew about him was bullshit, the movie star said: he meant what she might have read.

I don't read, Slotnik said.

He had been the winningest quarterback in Chalkton, and won a scholarship to the Big Ten university outside Indianapolis known for its football team and theater department. Had he not suffered an injury that first week and limped his way to auditions, or met Teddy Fine, soon to be in self-exile in Key West, a fading professor emeritus now known for his key lime pie and wicked mojitos but at the time very much the head of the theater department and the only man powerful enough to pluck a hobbled freshman to keep for his own, he might not be here now.

---

the needlepoint bolsters dedicated to the original founders of this particular congregation, names Abigail and the others had gleaned through much research and from the church cemetery.

He of course understood Teddy Fine's real intentions, but he had held Teddy back, he explained to Slotnik.

Uh-huh, Slotnik said.

I'd like you to engage, the movie star said.

How so? Slotnik said.

Speak, the movie star said. Say something. Give me your opinion. Argue with me. Tell me what I don't know, what it means.

I don't give answers, Slotnik said.

Understood, the movie star said.

But let's start with your name, Slotnik said. Is it real?

No, the movie star said.

I like it, Slotnik said.

Thank you.

So, what's it really?

What?

Your name?

I don't say.

Uh-huh.

It's not anything.

Uh-huh.

# XXXIII

In the glorious colors of a cooler autumn, Jules stood at the doorway home from law school, just a subway ride away, Columbia University, and Abe could not have been more proud. Abe, his skin waxy and cold to the touch, lay in their bed. Marie slept on the daybed in the sitting room. She was to give him the morphine in the syringe, a milliliter or a centimeter or something; every morning she drew the liquid to the line as the hospice nurse had shown her. The hospice nurse said every two hours but Marie gave the morphine every half hour and what the hell, she said to herself more than once, what the hell.

Jules has come home! He stands in the doorway, the light behind. He has his laundry, his socks; he wears a new beard.

"Jules!" she says.

"Hi, Mom," he says.

He walks past and drops his backpack on the Queen Anne chair next to the walnut sideboard, his keys in the cloisonné bowl, the china one with the Chinaman in blue. Do you know why the Huns went west? she can still hear Abe asking Jules as a little boy, the two at the kitchen table over Jules's history books. The Great Wall. It actually stopped them!

Jules gets into the bed with his father. He is careful not to touch his father's legs or his knees or his shoulder. He is careful to lie on his side. Where Abe stares is difficult to see. Perhaps Very Grand speaks only the language of the dead, or the near dead, or perhaps he is just in his morphine dream.

"I have a joke, Dad," Jules says. "Are you ready for a joke?"

He had always been a sensitive boy. There were never many friends. His mother and father were his friends, and then, mostly, his father. His father now lies in the bed, his face sunken, gaunt, his skin pale and stretched across his skull so that he already looks a skeleton.

"You're going to like this one," Jules says, touching his father's hand.

Abe smiles and if his eyes could be bright they would be bright.

"So," Jules says. He is very close to his father's ear, though careful. The pain is terrible, he knows. Like breaking bones, the doctor has told Marie and she, unable not to say it to Jules, had said it to Jules and then immediately regretted it—after all these years such a good secret keeper, such a good stoic and this?*

"Ready?" Jules says. And almost imperceptibly but percep-

---

*Not until Remembrance Day, when Jules had the school assignment, did she ever say a word: why speak of such things? Remembrance Day not to her liking, Marie said. This, now, who we are, she said. Onward, she said, Jules baffled by his mother's sudden anger. It was the neighbors I most despised, she told him: St. Claire's idiot boys; the widow with the pony and the milk cart. They took my mother's loom. Jules listened and then drew a picture of a pony pulling a milk cart, a loom, or how his mother described to him a loom, in the milk cart, the perspective skewed, the loom misshapen, curved as an angel's wing and too large—he had been very young. He had never seen a loom or a milk cart.

tibly Abe nods. He loves his boy. It is as if his body is already a shell he could burst from with the light of his love for his boy.

"Why did Noah not take any apples on the ark?" Jules says.

Do his eyes flicker? Jules wants to know. Is that a flicker?

I can't tell, Marie says. I think I imagine it sometimes and then I think no, there's definitely something.

I think that's a flicker, Jules says.

He leans in to kiss Abe's hollow cheek and Abe bursts with light.

"Because God said only pairs," Jules says.

Abe's smile is the smile he wears for certain voices—his son's voice and his wife's voice at times. He was a happy man, Marie thinks, watching her son and her husband lie in the bed, side by side, her son straight with not touching, with carefulness, her son the height and length of his father, as handsome, all Abe except for his eyes: her eyes.

He will not stay for dinner or for wine. He has a class tomorrow and he has promised his roommate something. He will be back in the morning, or maybe the day after tomorrow—his filthy sneakers on the bed and after all that, Abe, after we've told him so many times—but Abe will already be gone and so this is it: "because God said only pairs." A punch line; a joke—last words overrated, Jules said first to his roommate, then his boyfriend, testing how it sounds, how it might sound, though it sounds like shit, Jules said afterward. It sounds like total shit.

# XXXIV

There were still books. Elizabeth would read them for hours, forgetting the time. Dinner came and went like in children's stories, plates gone cold as the blue dusk fell or the sun rose. Beggar girls—Chinese, Japanese, Vietnamese—sought answers from the Man in the Moon. They followed their golden dragons, believing in golden stairways that led straight up. The girls were driven by desperation: their parents starving in the Forgotten Village, existing on two or three grains of rice after their days' labor. The girls would speak to the golden dragons, who would go along, protecting them from the various obstacles they encountered along the way, ferocious animals or unscrupulous merchants. They were innocent girls who believed in the dreams of the night before or week, sleeping on pine needles in the Forgotten Forest. All they had to do was get out of the Forest. They believed in that, though their parents, convinced of their deaths, had gone gray as sheets as they poked holes in the muddy swamps, planting another meager rice crop. Sometimes one had a lucky copper bowl. Sometimes one had a premonition, or an encounter with a magical goldfish.

The bird in its tiny cage, hopping on one scrawny claw as the other reached to pluck the scroll: the fortune.

Tell us what it means, the destitute parent asked of the copper bowl, the magical goldfish. Tell us when it will end, or begin.

She yawned and rose, hungry or not at all. She read and read and the years passed as if nothing had ever happened, as if no one had been lost to the world, taken into the water. Her sixteenth birthday at the summer place in that great, high-ceilinged room in the White Mountains, a fire in the fireplace, alone. She had lied to be here, where she worked in the dining room clearing tables and washing dishes: seventeen years of age, minimum. Yes, yes, she had said to the employer, a Mrs. Something who wasn't born yesterday, who knew which end was up. And now, day off and raining, Elizabeth read the book she had brought from home, from the box marked FREE. She yawned: Happy Birthday to me, she said under her breath.

Out the window the lake stretched and steamed toward forever, its borders edged with cattails, clogged with the felled, waterlogged stumps of beaver dams. There were loon and warm-blooded mammals, nocturnal, hiding. On the long graceful roots of the water lilies egg sacs that would hatch in days: tadpoles. Just last night she had heard an owl and the boy in her bed had said, Is that an owl?

She thought how that sounded, *the boy in her bed*. She thought how that would feel to say it: more than wanting to *do* it, she had wanted to *say* it, to name it, to say she had. But the doing: she could still feel his hands in certain places and she wished them back, wished him back though this was not his day off. Tomorrow's my birthday, she had told him, and he, the coolest in the pack, the long-banged boy, had said, Let's celebrate, and someone had something from home, illegal and sweet. It made her feel old and reckless and she had let the boy unbutton

her jeans and put his hand there, and she had twisted around
so he would put his hand into her, and she had felt as if all of
her might puddle into butter like Sambo, one of the stories she
remembers though mostly the look of its cover and illustrations,
the black boy and the ferocious tiger.

"You are a tiger," the boy had said, as if he were reading her
mind. He has taken off all her clothes and his, and he pushes
into her in the place his hand kneaded and warmed though now
it feels too small for him and he is no longer here anyway. He's
somewhere else, jerking on top of her.

The boy smells delicious and feels soft as she feels. A summer night though cool. The lights are out and they are in her
bed and the room is the maid's room, chamber pot on the
bureau as if for flowers but there are no flowers here, only stiff
green pine and dried brown needles and stones to stub your toe
if you skinny-dip and they will, they do—she wants to wash the
boy out of her, there had been so much of him—but it is cold,
cold in the shadows of the overhanging spruce, her feet sunk in
the mud, a mire of decomposing leaves that had once composed
the autumn and the spring, that had once composed Molly; now
only the green of summer, these woods, the children, the teenagers—a beautiful boy and a beautiful girl asleep in the narrow
bed meant for one, their hair still wet with lake, a fishy smell,
the dusty, mothballed blanket pulled to their chins, their eyes
sweet with sleep.

The beautiful boy has been here before but she has never
been and doesn't want to wake up, doesn't want to stir in case
the boy decides to leave too early. He has work to do. He must
deliver the ice to the iceboxes and new guests want sailing les-
sons. There will be another pretty girl in their company and he
will flirt, forgetting her for the afternoon or at least until dinner,
when the other staff wink as he sets down his tray beside hers.

What's up, he'll say, and she'll know, just by that, which way the wind blows. (East-west, he told the family, smiling at the new pretty girl, a blonde in a string bikini, pancake flat but amazing turquoise eyes. She loved him immediately, the coolest boy, long-banged, dull.)

I read a great book today, she'll say.

Yeah? he says, forgetting her birthday, but then the bell rings as the guest who caught the big fish steps from the kitchen holding it high above his head and the other guests in the dining room and the staff and even the cook come out from the kitchen to applaud.

The boy's name Teddy, she remembers. She wrote him letters and he wrote her one.*

It's usually smooth as glass! Elizabeth shouts to her father, there to see her, a surprise, the two now in the motorboat, a whaler, thirty-horsepower, a putt-putt to take him to Grizzly Cove, where he might catch a big fish everyone will applaud at dinner. The lake whips around them as he drives the boat, as the boat smacks the rough, the whitecaps, then slams down hard again on the black water, slams down again and again, the waves rising up to take her under, she knows, to take her down.

---

*Last year she looked him up online and found photographs: the boy all grown with his family. They stood six in a row near a lake and she wondered if it were the same lake, if Teddy had returned to the camp as a guest, caught a fish or two, sailed with his daughters, hiked the mountain that rose up to shadow the whole or to pierce the storm clouds that always came in so quickly, roughing the lake water that usually, in the early evening, was smooth as glass.

# XXXV

The keys, if she's ever wondered, are to storage bins in the basement, Sid Morris tells Marie. You cannot believe the junk people leave behind—all their masterpieces! Years of work! Pouf! They're gone and I'm left with the crap of their labor.

She hasn't asked, she does not say.

They stand in Sid Morris's office in the empty School of Inspired Arts, the Yoga Center on the third floor holding some kind of meditation retreat. Scores of scruffy men and women shuffle up and down the stairs. They must have just let them out for a cigarette, Sid Morris says.

Imagine sitting all day saying nothing, Marie says.

Death would be more interesting, Sid Morris says. Tried it once. Meditation, not death, but what's the difference? You should hear the idiotic questions: "If I'm breathing out my left nostril and I accidentally breathe out my right, is that a problem?"

Marie laughs. She does not know what she expected showing up on a vacant Saturday; she had come to tell him that she is leaving her house after all, that she does not want Sid Morris to embark on the journey west and find her gone.

It happens to the best of us, Sid Morris says, looking down.

He checks a book of some kind, a ledger filled in pale ink. She watches as he draws a line through what she sees is her name in a long list of others and now x-ed like his calendar days—before noon?—the month almost passed, late May. Outside, the weather has turned glorious, lilac and rose.

"It's a beautiful day," she says. "You should get out."

"Is that so?" he says. He leans against his battered metal desk, Henry's canvas behind him somehow mounted to the cinderblock wall. A heater clicks on and off in the corner though it is too warm and the windows are open, the air sweet or perhaps the Chinese are cooking. Chopin again on the radio, she thinks, remembering aloud the day with Simone, the snowflakes melting on the wooden floor.

Debussy, Sid Morris says. Compliments Helen. She thought I might be interested. Cézanne's musical counterpart, she says. An Impressionist, she says.

I see, Marie says.

Our resident intellectual, Sid Morris says.

Debussy?

Helen, he says.

Oh, she says. She listens to the music awhile, they both do. A lost sound retrieved from an archive of lost sounds. Debussy himself on the piano—restored, polished—so that suddenly the great composer sits in the room at his instrument, the two of them like guests. The rest of the building has gone quiet as well, the weekend meditation retreat back to its group sit. From time to time, a bell chimes, the only other sound besides Claude at his piano, concentrating. Above Sid Morris, behind his desk, the completed Brooklyn Bridge spans the wall; Marie thinks of how Sid Morris guided the brush in Simone's hand, shading this, foreshortening that, and how afterward Simone had said that even though his breath smelled rank it had felt good to be held. It had felt very good.

Katherine hardly hugs back, she said. And you remember how Henry was in so much pain.

Eventually, the music stops.

"The bridge looks beautiful," Marie says to fill the gap, because it does: anchored to the mighty river, the steel of it against a darkening sky that showed, in certain places, the possibility of blue, a color, Sid Morris once told them, most primal, not of the soil but of something more—the rock at the center of the earth. Cézanne knew this, he had said. Cézanne understood blue, he said.

"A work in progress," he says, smiling.

He steps out from his battered desk and he is very close, as close as he sometimes stood behind her before, watching. What she painted she never fully understood, nor did she care. It was the paint is all; the smell of the paint and the color of the paint and the paint on the brush; she was trying to make something of the way life *felt*. This is what she could never say. The way life felt, or that particular moment of life—if it could be cleared of everything else, if it could be seen and heard and *felt*: the light through the filthy windows, the sighs of the tattooed model, Sid Morris behind her, watching.

"I'm very sorry to see you go," Sid Morris says. "I have enjoyed your company."

"Well," she says.

"I would have snuck back but the last time your son gave me the evil eye."

"Did he?"

"Someone did. Handsome chap. Well dressed."

"That was his friend, Larry," Marie says.

"He didn't tell you?"

"No," Marie says. "But he doesn't say much to me. I think he and Jules have had a falling-out."

"Jules?" Sid Morris says.

"My son," Marie says, understanding how little Sid Morris knows at all, or remembers.

He guides her toward the broken-down divan; she suddenly shaky—it comes on, from time to time, out of nowhere.

"Mrs. Shivers," he says.

"Mrs. Shiver-Me-Timbers," she says, sitting. He'll find the fringed Renaissance scarf the model wears for the draft, thrown out from the prop shop across the street in late autumn about the time you and your sidekick showed up, Sid Morris says. I say silk she says polyester mix and it itches but she uses it anyway, he says. What a complaintnik! It's too hot! It's too cold! I need coffee! I need air! I can't breathe! This is giving me a leg cramp! My God! Sid Morris says, wrapping Marie in the fringed scarf, tucking it around her frail shoulders—she looks to have shrunk since he last saw her.

The fringed scarf smells of the model's smell, she tells him, or what she remembers of the model's smell: a little moldy.

"Hah!" Sid Morris says, but he knows what she really means is those were happy days; happy, happy days.

Sid Morris lumps sugar into his tea and stirs too loudly; she can see from here white whiskers in his ear and a tiny plastic ball tucked there for hearing. He tells her what he hasn't wanted to say to anyone. He is in the same straits. They are clearing the whole building out. They have offered more than he can turn down for his lease and so. He shrugs. *"Va bene,"* he says, dunking a crumbling cookie into his cup. "I'd be a fool not to take it. Besides," he says, gesturing to the suitcase. "I'm already packed."

He slurps his tea. "Veritas offered the apartment over her garage in Baltimore, God forbid. Maybe there and Vero Beach for winter. Seasonal rental. Rauschenberg's light or used to be. I don't know what's happened to the light.

"Anyway, the City is no longer the City," he says, looking elsewhere.

# XXXVI

It is as if she, too, is trapped by ice, Elizabeth says. A wall of ice, she says. And where is Pete? Slotnik says. Ben? She has been seeing Slotnik for a very long time. Once even, Slotnik came to dinner. It was entirely against protocol but there she was at the front door. Screw protocol, she had said. She ate roast chicken and admired the wood floors, the ones that dated back to Lincoln's presidency.

I'm holding his hand, Elizabeth says. In this one we're all holding hands.

# XXXVII

It did look a little like love, Sid Morris told Gretchen. It looked a lot like love, he said. She wanted it so. love. She had come all this way. She had made her way here for love, she said, stoned.

She was always stoned.

Sid Morris pressed the bumpy raised scar, purple, with his calloused thumb.

A lot like love, Sid Morris repeated to his beautiful Gretchen. She had once been so beautiful. So fucking beautiful, Sid Morris would say, and he did, to anyone who would still listen.

But the fever got worse, ate her body like a cheese. She shivered so she could not stop and the doctor, the young resident, had already disappeared to treat the drunk with the gash on his temple, a comatose teenager.

Gretchen died that night. The next morning Sid Morris stood on his mother's doorstep with an infant Veritas in his arms and asked forgiveness and she gave it, taking the baby in for a night, for a week, for years.*

---

*Goddess of Truth, his mother would say to the question, the first one always asked from the other women pushing carriages on the boardwalk. Daughter

He buried Gretchen in Queens, in the cemetery everyone passes on their way out of town, the rows and rows and rows and rows. It had been his idea to bring Marie to meet her. I want you to meet her, he had said. They rode out in a taxi, Sid Morris pulling crumpled dollar bills, spilling some, from his jacket pockets, the fare steep.

The last time it was five dollars, he told the driver with a wink.

They walked through the cemetery to Gretchen's grave. It took some time to find it, everything so green. Alive. The birds were singing high in the trees, calling out to one another, mates and chums looking for company. A beautiful day. You couldn't deny, Sid Morris said, helping Marie along—her hobbling like an old woman, she said—you couldn't deny it a beautiful day.

"Beautiful," she said, smiling. She felt as if she hadn't seen the sun in years.

Earlier he had confessed the truth: they had closed him down without warning—violations, penalties, the outrage! The rent tripled overnight or maybe the entire place for condos, more of those glass towers. Have you see them? Needles! No wonder it's raining! The hubris! Jesus! God help us! Who lives in glass houses?

Stone throwers? Marie said.

What? Sid said.

People who will live in glass houses, she said.

He looked at her.

---

of Saturn, Mother of Virtue—Veritas, a goddess so shy she would not allow herself to be seen. She hid in water, at the bottom of a well. At this the other women would look down and admire again the baby with the odd name from the mother dead from drugs, the baby who stared back at them, unblinking: Goddess of Truth, Daughter of Saturn, Mother of Virtue.

That's it? he said. That's all you've got?

And for this, for all she cannot explain, she takes his hand; they sit on the broken-down divan, the heat kicking on though it's already warm, the low hum of the collective Om downstairs rising, buoying their old spirits as well, perhaps. Sid Morris her friend, Marie thinks, her last friend.

She has wanted to touch him since before she can remember and now she does. He pulls her close and she can see the dark eyes and loose skin and the places where he hasn't shaved and his eyebrows and all of him arranged like a kit of parts, his breath rank with tobacco smoke. And it surprises her and does not surprise her that he kisses her then, again and again, and what she feels from the softness of his lips and the strength in his arms, holding her, is the answer to Simone's question that we are never, truly, old, in our hearts, old.*

---

*These kisses she will remember at her own death, much sooner than expected although the one constant of death, the director of the retirement home is quick to point out to Jules, is that it comes calling at inopportune times. The director is as oily as the lines he speaks, and it is all Jules can do to get in and get out, Jules on this mission alone, Larry long ago returned to California, the two having terminated their relationship although Larry does, decently, send flowers as soon as he hears, flowers that arrive several days after the fact, given the inclement weather, and atmospheric disruptions in general: the no-fly zone temporarily in place over the Dakotas. Still. The flowers are revived to good health and last through the funeral, a private affair, since Marie would have never wanted a fuss, Jules knew. She wanted to be cremated, she wrote in a letter she had left behind in the cloisonné bowl and addressed to Jules, knowing he would find it as he cleared the rest of everything out. She left her worldly possessions to her adored son, Jules Lincoln Frank, named, she writes in a footnote to the single sheet of paper of her will, a footnote in the shaky, fading ink of her hand, for the two men who saved her life—the forgotten photographer Jules Gradeau, who forged her papers out, and her beloved husband, Abraham Lincoln Frank.

It is only then, reading his mother's addition, that Jules breaks down for all he has lost and all he will never know and for the beauty of who she was, his mother, Marie.

But first, Sid Morris's kisses: Marie feels Sid Morris's kisses in the dark, her eyes closed, dreaming. Is she dreaming, again? She liked his eyes, mostly: he reminded her of a boy she had known in London, one of the sweet soldiers she sometimes danced with, the boys who bought her gum, stockings if they could pinch them. The boys were on leave or about to go— this near the end of it, when the rubble you did not want to step through you stepped through in the morning on your way; the feral dog and occasionally or maybe only once the fingers of a hand in its jaw. You would walk anywhere just to get to blue, the blue sky—did she know blue? Sid Morris had asked, not the color of land but the color of the sea—walk anywhere to escape the war, the constant disaster, emergency. Once she found a cantaloupe in Russell Square. Another time the ruins of a bookstore, a single wall of books standing, untouched. She pulled Dickens from a shelf.

Maybe it's a dream and maybe it's not but Marie kisses Sid Morris back. She lets him hold her and she kisses him and then, opening her eyes, she sees that it has not been Sid Morris at all, but Abe. Abe is here. He's come home and now here he is: standing right in front of her. He smiles in the way of Abe and she smiles back to see him. She was waiting, she does not say. She was beginning to feel all alone.

# XXXVIII

Flights have been canceled. They'll be out tomorrow if they're lucky, though there's no accounting for this crazy weather. Yesterday hail. A few odds and ends at home and then back, again. So much to do but for now, a tornado somewhere: Midwest or lower—farther south. Near Texas but not on the border, north.

All right, Larry says.

An omen, Jules says.

Oh God, Larry says. Here goes, Larry says.

There's a consensus but still people do not believe there's a consensus. They think it's an act of God.

God is dead, Elizabeth says. If nothing else, she remembers her Nietzsche.

Is that Shaw? Larry asks.

Nietzsche, Elizabeth says. They have invited her down so she will not be alone in this weather: the wind howling, the subways closed—the storm appearing out of nowhere. Everyone advised to stay precisely where they are: Pete at work in his shelter-in-place, Ben at Progressive K–8 in his shelter-in-place. It's a Citywide lockdown: shut the windows, bolt the doors.

And tornadoes, Jules says.

Enough! Larry says.

I mean, yes, there have always been tornadoes, but did you see this one? Did you see the news? Whole parking lots, everything, crushed. We looked like ants swarming over it.

Aren't you glad you're here, Elizabeth?

Where else would I be? Elizabeth says. She's trying not to get worked up. She's trying to look on the bright side.

It will pass, Marie had said, opening the door wide for Elizabeth, who had said yes, she would feel a lot better in company.

I love you, Pete texted.

I love you, too, she texted back.

At the door Elizabeth held up the fishing tackle box Pete had put together, the one he labeled CONTINGENCIES. I've got contingencies, she yelled to the boys in the kitchen.

And we've got chips! Larry called back.

Now they sit around Marie's old table drinking the rest of the sherry Jules found in the Antoinette cabinet—not just the bottle but the cut-crystal tumblers and the snifters and the sterling silver nut bowl Larry insisted on polishing with toothpaste before the almonds were procured. Circa 1973, these almonds, he said. Nuts don't get old, Marie said, to which they all laughed.

"In honor of Great-Aunt Eleanor. Elegance at all times," Jules had said, pouring.

"Cheers!" Marie said.

"I feel like Marlene Dietrich," Larry said, clinking his glass. "I need a turban."

They've already had a lot; they've already had enough. In the ancient dust on the sherry bottle they scrawl their names, the date. Just in case no one finds them. Larry was here, Larry writes. From the sherry to the wine, bottles a thousand years old. There is not much else to do but wait it out and drink. Anyway, Marie says, in the place where she is going they will require a note of approval for alcohol with dinner. In the place where she's going she will have to share a room, and she will have to share a living room, and she will have to share a dining room, and when she gets infirm, if she gets infirm, she will have to share an infirm dining room.

"At least there's company," Jules says, watching as the first gusts bend the cherry tree to the ground and fling it up again, its blossoms hurtled like so much window confetti. Make it rain, he would say to his father. Pink rain best, he would say.

"Look," he says now.

And they do. They watch the miracle of it all: how the tree does not snap but bends this way and that, throwing off its glorious pink, a survivor.

"Onward," Marie says, watching.

What If your life suddenly gives out on you?
What If your home sinks into the sea?

# XXXIX

The e-mail went out at noon of the probability for Sudden Weather—this moniker a new subcategory of disaster coined in the Midwest from the microbursts and combustible clouds that magically appeared out of nothing, like Dorothy's tornado, Sudden Weather now one of the many disasters listed on the New York preparedness website.

Shelter-in-Place activated, the e-mail subject line read. The text, as per the directive of Wayne Arden, the new interim, interim principal of Progressive K–8, a series of bullet points. Declarative sentences get to the heart of the matter, Wayne Arden had said at his Introductory Wine & Cheese, sparsely attended by the Applicant families and Vicky and Matty Tange. He stood in front of a PowerPoint and slowly read the declarative sentences, as if the gathered did not know how to read them themselves. He read the lines as if they were poetry. He had written them earlier with the help of Bernice Stilton, she the brains and balls of the operation, he understood from the start.*

---

*Yet never in her lifetime would she forgive herself for what she believed was the responsibility she bore for the sudden departure of Margaret Constantine,

Know that precautions have been taken.

Know that Progressive K–8's Shelter-in-Place is in place.

Know that your children are safe with us.

Know that your children have been drilled.

Know that thousands of dollars have been spent.

Know that we are doing all this to keep your children alive.

This may actually be the big one, Jules says; he's consulting his device although connections are fuzzy. The new mayor sounds

---

PhD, for New Zealand, a woman she considered a friend at an age when friendships seemed almost too much to bear, given the accumulations and disappointments in a life, given what would eventually be lost. Many nights she returned to the drinks the two had shared at that sticky bar. How she had told Dr. Constantine about her oldest boy, Lenin, and dancing with Frank Sinatra, and how the next morning, or maybe the one after that, she had shown Margaret Constantine the way to Google Earth: Go on, she'd urged. Give it a try.

She had stood behind Constantine and watched as she typed in Ariel's address, watched as the camera pivoted on the satellite in the very dark of space, above the atmosphere, even, though she couldn't be sure of that, but somewhere far, far away, as high as the stars in their distant, fiery places, though what we see of any of it is already in the past. She and Margaret Constantine had watched as the camera zoomed in on what looked like brown swatches of nothing and then rows and rows of houses and then what looked like water and forests and then, finally, a bungalow of sorts, something built from wood and painted white, the banana fronds and ferns that shaded its front walk grown to almost the size of the house itself. The screen door looked propped open by a brick, or a rock; within the house barely perceptible movement and shifting shadows. Perhaps the play of all that vegetation or perhaps a person—her daughter?—sitting at a table, in a chair.

"Should I go?" Margaret Constantine had asked. And to this Bernice had said, "You must go."

nervous. He says it's best to get out. If you choose to stay, he can no longer protect you. If you choose to stay, the mayor has said, good luck. Jules has heard all this on the radio; he passes along the news as Marie pours Elizabeth more wine and winks. Elizabeth smiles and closes her eyes, trying to calm her heart; in times like this she pictures the boat her father drove over the rough lake toward Grizzly Cove, the two of them inside it, the whitecaps swamping them in fishy lake water, drowning them, practically. "What are you made of?" her father had shouted into the wind. "Show me what you're made of, Lizzie!" he had shouted.*

---

*The years pass quickly, decades, even, accumulations of conversations and interruptions and good dinners and drinks, moves to houses first empty then filled to bursting—Marie's brownstone to a brick colonial in Rye, higher ground, where the family suffers the rest of Ben's teenage years.

He smashes the car against the flagpole and walks away with just a scrape: a miracle or someone watching over him. His first date a girl from a faraway Asian country he will grow to love and marry the day after graduation.

Elizabeth and Pete follow their son and his new wife to Canada given the forecasts, offering to babysit the grandchildren, three, every chance they get, Pete especially adept at getting the grandchildren to sleep, Elizabeth listening to the stories he spins out of thin air, leaning against the doorway, watching him, surprised each time a little by her love for this man—for their fiftieth anniversary she gives him a novel, *The Possessed*. The youngest grandson is Elizabeth's particular favorite, a boy who will not look her in the eye or speak but who, every once in a while, claps and squeals at the top of his lungs. He is a handsome boy who grows to be the spitting image of his grandfather.

Outside the drought turns the green hills and the green valleys to mud and then dust, crumbling the earth to so many sand cakes. You used to call them sand cakes, remember? Elizabeth says. The old sandbox Mrs. Frank let you use in the backyard in Chelsea? She takes a walk along the cliff with Ben. She leans on his arm as he steadies her. Your father would have liked the view, she tells him, and her son says, He would have very much. The

Shelter can be had for a song at PS 11, where the Gifted and Talented kindergartners—the ones who last week sold the trucked-in vegetables from the farm in Staten Island on the school steps, their handmade signs adorable, their enthusiasm contagious: ZUCCHINI! LETTUCE! STRAWBERRIES!—unpack the pre-packed emergency kits: fresh towels and toiletries they will hand to their frantic neighbors when the rain begins. The rain is beginning and no one quite knows what will happen next. This may be a real emergency, someone says on the broken, staticky television Larry keeps on in Marie's kitchen. He turned it on for company

---

view is the Pacific Ocean, as constant as the North Star or the Insomniac on the ninth floor. Do you remember the Insomniac on the ninth floor? Elizabeth asks. When we lived in Chelsea? That building in back—the ugly one: he never turned his light off. Not once. Any time of night you'd look out and see the ninth-floor light. Mrs. Frank, do you remember her? Marie? Lovely woman. She called him the Insomniac of the ninth floor. She let you use the sandbox.

I remember her, Ben says, steadying Elizabeth over a particularly deep fissure. There are signs everywhere: AT YOUR OWN RISK. FALLING BANK.

Falling bank? Ben had said earlier. It should say, Failing bank.

Failing bank, Elizabeth said. That's funny, she said. Now she grips Ben's arm to get over the particularly deep fissure. Everything is at their own risk; there are no longer any protections in the field, landscapes awash with disclaimers. The National Park Service condo project, even, she has read, requires a certificate of noninsurance before money can change hands: fire, flood, tornado, earthquake. The Pacific Ocean roils and froths below, breaking over the rocky outcrops and small islands just beyond, the remnants of Highway 1 that appear only at low tide.

"Maybe there were just too many ghosts," she says. "Maybe he just needed to keep the lights on."

"Who?" Ben says.

"The Insomniac of the ninth floor," she says.

"Maybe," Ben says, his hand on her bony elbow, negotiating. "Maybe."

as he packed the last of Marie's kitchen things. Might as well pack, he says. Keep busy, he says.

The sailboats in the Hudson tear against their moorings while above them helicopters drone, here and over the East River, the shoals of Staten Island and the New Jersey boardwalks, charred and still burning from last year's fires.

"This is ridiculous," Jules says, turning off his device. He can no longer get any bars, the system overloaded.

"What about the TV?" Larry says. He has bitten his fingernails to the quick and now works his cuticles.

"A joke," Jules says.

"It works," Larry says.

Mayors sit around a wooden table, arguing.

"It's a rerun," Jules says. "That's Koch. Koch is dead. This is something else entirely, a different emergency."

"I wish I could understand what they're saying," Larry says.

"It's a rerun!" Jules says.

"It's soothing," Larry says. He sits very still, watching the old mayors who admit they cannot predict what's coming next discuss what's coming next.

# XL

Very Grand is not amused. Who knows when the water will reach her slippered feet? Already her toes are moist and cracked and now the water rises from the basement, entirely flooded so that the hot-water heater swirls with the washer and the dryer and the mud that once, remarkably, they packed with horsehair and straw and molded into bricks. The mud bricks are layers of sludge, actually, studded with two-bit-piece coins and arrowheads.

Imagine it! Abe had said. These foundations laid as the Civil War raged!

# XLI

Abe wore his blanket like a wrap, his bones honeycombed, always cold. The doctor said the pain was such he felt his bones broken, every one, this the reason then for the amounts of morphine, increasing, to take him away from the pain of broken bones. He slept and slept and in the few times he waked she groomed him, brushing his sparse hair with the silver brush with the mother-of-pearl handle, a baby brush, his intricate, carved initials. She polished the brush and laid it next to the silver comb on the silver tray, all of one set, all of one piece, next to their bed. His hair white, thin; the blanket white, thin, loosely knitted by Jules, practicing. She read him the books they had loved as he slept. She watched him sleep: his hollowed-out eyes, his skeletal teeth. Very Grand looked on. She wished it over and then she wished it never over. She wished his heart would stop. She wished her heart would stop. She rubbed lotion on his old feet, the toenails cracked, greenish. When he smiled, he would always smile, she traced his beautiful smile lines with the tip of her finger and thought how long it had been since she looked so closely at her husband, a happy man. Marry a happy man, her mother had said. This she did remember.

His body turned to something else entirely, a gnome, a hobbit from the garden, an illustration, something Great-Aunt Elea-nor might have collected, fissures in his skin already cracked and cracking, and when he died she did not want to sit with it, his body. She wanted it gone. He was no longer there: he had disap-peared. Where? she asked the undertaker. They had come with her phone call, the ones on Thompson Street that had been there forever. Mr. Winowsky, he introduced himself. The owner. This a family business.

He introduced himself at the front door, his two sons, big lugs, hovered behind in Yankees caps.

She showed them the room and then she stepped aside as they lifted the body no longer Abe onto a stretcher and covered him. In books, in films she had seen, the widow sits beside the bed holding the hand of the dead spouse, talking to the dead spouse, refusing the last good-bye with the corpse. She could understand none of it. Abe has disappeared, she told Mr. Win-owsky. I have no idea where he's gone.

Do you have family? Mr. Winowsky wanted to know; his face gleamed with sweat though his sons were doing the labor.

A son. He's on his way. I called you first.

Mr. Winowsky looked puzzled at this, as if she had upset the natural order of grief.

Far?

Columbia, she said. University.

Oh, Mr. Winowsky said. He appeared to take inventory of the foyer, the grandfather clock and its hands, stuck, the bowl on the walnut sideboard; the small alabaster lamp. If the lights were completely out, she could tell him, the alabaster lamp would glow a beautiful yellow, a light made from stone.

The boys negotiated the hallway with Abe's body, covered in a sheet. Abe on his way out the door of their grand adventure. Good-bye, Abe, she thinks but does not say.

# XLII

Time will pass as time will pass. The City still stands. One year becomes five, then ten. Children grow like weeds as do the sycamores shedding their rough bark with the warmer weather, dirty trees, the residents say, sweeping up after them. The residents have lived here forever or they have just moved in. The residents are thinking of leaving, or they have just arrived.

On the High Line the high school kids practice their samba; there is no more room in the cafeterias for dance and besides, tests are being taken, scores tallied—the fate of the untutored millions. In front of the dancers, on the billboard, the underwear model looms over a skeleton in lace, his erection obvious. And what of the machinations of his mind? thinks one of the dancers, a boy who has recently learned the word *machination* and is eager to use it until, called to pay attention, he loses the word entirely, dance not his forte and his concentration gone weak, he tells the instructor, a woman who rallied the principal to sign the forms to allow the teenagers to pass out the doors of the school, doors guarded now by dropouts hired by a security firm for less than minimum wage, registered guns clipped to their belts. Not your forte, tough shit, the woman who rallied the principal told the boy. You're going to dance as if it's the last thing, she said. And so he does, and so they all do; they dance as if it's the last thing, high above the crowds of Chelsea, the throngs beneath the High Line and west, in the rebuilt parks along the newly shored landfill and west, on the concrete, fireproofed pier where once the banana boats docked and now the next batch of toddlers ride the new donkey carousel, screaming at the tops of their tiny lungs.

But this is in five years, maybe ten. Now, here, the seminary bells toll, marking the beginning of one hour or, possibly, the end of another.